Miracle

Phillipa Vincent-Connolly

Pen Press

First published in Great Britain by Pen Press

All paper used in the printing of this book has been made from wood grown in managed, sustainable forests.

ISBN: 978-1-78003-496-6

Printed and bound in the UK
Pen Press is an imprint of
Indepenpress Publishing Limited
25 Eastern Place
Brighton
BN2 1GJ

A catalogue record of this book is available from
the British Library

Cover design by Jacqueline Abromeit

For my Mum, Anna Witherington, who passed away 30th October 2011. And for Jane Goldman, without whose inspiration and enthusiasm, I would never have finished it.

To all disabled women out there, who dare to dream – just believe in yourself and take no notice of anyone else!

Author's note

৯ One ৶

I had never given any thought to who I would end up dating, let alone marrying – it just hadn't crossed my mind. With my mum, Rachael, always pursuing romance then perhaps, eventually, I should consider the possibility. Life through my eyes wasn't a fairytale; happy endings just didn't exist. Not in my world at least. Mum viewed everything through rose-tinted glasses, almost as if she'd stepped out of a fairy story. I did not. Being me was not like being a normal teenage girl.

As I drove home in the winter dusk, the rain came down in sheets and the dazzle of oncoming headlights was intensified by the reflections from the wet road. Switching on the demister, I sighed as the realisation hit me that I would be trapped in this twisted body for the rest of my life. Accepting it was the hard part and I guessed it always would be. I felt like I'd been stored in the wrong body. Was this how a transsexual felt? Whatever, it was not my idea of fun.

I should be used to it by now, but I still get upset when people stare at me like I'm some freak of nature who shouldn't even be out. Earlier today, as I grabbed a sandwich from the corner shop with my friend, Amelia, a couple of young lads were even grimacing and pointing at me as well. Their amused expressions said it all as I limped across the street, stumbling over kerbstones and trying to avoid the humiliation of falling.

This small town was not the easiest place for me to get around, with its uneven paving slabs, shops with steps but no handrails, and a car park too far away from the amenities. I had only just made it to the car this evening.

The pain that had plagued me all day almost subsided as I sank into the driving seat. As the pain eased, so the burning and tingling of finally being off my feet began, never allowing me to forget who I was.

My head pounded with rage, as my mind wrestled with the torment of the strain and pain involved in simple physical actions that everyone else took for granted. I hated my body, and my mind was repulsed as its passenger. How I wished I could be "normal" – to be able to run, wear killer heels and walk with a sexy wiggle, rather than the demeaning waddle I was forced to perform to get from A to B! You would have thought I'd be used to it, having been like this since birth, but I wasn't, and doubted I ever would. Mine was a low self-esteem and nothing would or could dissuade me from that mindset. It was like a constant grey cloud over my head; a nightmare that would never end.

At the traffic lights I drew to a halt alongside an exclusive shoe boutique. The window display reflected the fashion for hot shoes of the moment; wickedly high heels with lots of embellishments and diamantés. Staring at my reflection in the glass, I imagined myself in the styles that I knew I'd never be able to wear.

Mum, of course, understood. She tried to say the right thing, or so she thought. However, it made no difference to my opinion of myself.

"It doesn't matter what you look like. It's what's inside that counts!"

It didn't reassure me, but what else could she say? Mum always tried to be kind and say the right thing, shielding me from the truth, in case it hurt me. She could be way too over-protective, almost suffocating, when she wanted to. She sounded like a cliché. I knew she meant well and I tried to make allowances for it, but we had many upsetting discussions about high heels and how I desperately wanted to be like my friends, to fit in, and wear the latest fashions in footwear.

The rain had turned to drizzle as I pulled up outside the house. Grabbing my stuff, I grappled with the umbrella and made for the front door, my small bunch of keys jangling as I pulled them from my coat pocket. It was quiet for a change as I turned the key in the lock of our three-bed semi. In Wimborne everyone knew everyone else's business, but I loved the small, semi-rural town with its beauty spots and glorious beaches which were a few miles down the road in the next town; its old-fashioned square, The King's Head Hotel, and the ancient Minster church.

I was greeted at the door by Gio, our golden Lhasa Apso. She hurled herself at me, yapping with excitement and licking my face. This was her welcoming ritual as soon as we opened the door. She reminded me of Mum, soft, silky smooth, well groomed, and sweet smelling. I tweaked the bow that tied her fringe up in a top knot. Mum must have taken her to the groomer's today. She felt heavy in my arms when I gave her cuddle and in return she flicked her pink tongue all over my face.

I peered round the kitchen door. Mum was home first today. "Hi, Mum!"

Steam rose from the bubbling saucepans that were on the hob. Mum looked tired; her face was pale and she looked anxious. Her long hair loosely tied up in a messy bun, minimal face on, with her lips showing just a hint of lippy. I guess I sometimes didn't appreciate how lonely she was. I had noticed she was starting to look older than her years – her lifestyle concerned me. Raising two girls alone was not the way she had planned to live her life. She was so lonely she was into online dating now. They weren't exactly the sort of men she wanted to meet or even hoped to meet. Personally, I believed the answer was to be introduced to someone she knew of, or who close friends knew – that way at least I knew she wouldn't end up with some anonymous weirdo!

"How are you? How was work?" I pecked her on the cheek. "You must have finished early? And how did you get on at the doctor's?"

"Okay. We had an INSET day that finished early, so that's why I'm home. I managed to get to the surgery but it was just a routine check-up. No problems, I promise." She sighed with feeling. "I'm just tired – tired of…" she paused, looking away from me, "…tired of everything. I miss male company you see, Orianna. Oh, don't get me wrong, I love you and your sister, but it doesn't compensate for having no man to love and look after."

"I know things are hard for you, Mum, but I'm glad you're okay. You know I worry about you."

She detected the concern in my voice and just gave me a half-smile. I went to the sink, ran some tap water into a glass and drank it back quickly.

"I'm just going to finish off my toile. My fashion homework is due in soon." Her familiar Amber scent washed over me as I gave her a hug.

"Yes, okay, love. Dinner will be about an hour. I am going out later, so you can go out with your friends tonight, if you like. Izzey's staying at her friend's, so there's no need to babysit."

"Thanks! Izzey's social life is busier than mine, especially for an 11-year-old girl. She's never here! You should get her to stay in sometimes, Mum."

Mum frowned. We'd been there before. Best to change the subject.

Ignoring her expression, I said, "Amelia and I were thinking of going to see *Breaking Dawn-Part 2* tonight at the cinema and perhaps meet up with Jack afterwards, if he's around."

"I wish you and Jack were dating. I like him and he's so cute with his blond spiky hairstyle."

"Oh, Mum! Not that again! We are friends. Trust me…it's better that way. You want to hook me up with someone just for the sake of it. Anyway, it's embarrassing talking about my love life, and after all, we only talk about your boyfriends and hot dates! I wish you'd get off those dating sites, out of those cheesy chat rooms. I know you have 26-year-olds asking you for dates; with that kind of age gap, its just wrong."

"Now, you stop your teasing, young lady, and show some respect. I am your mother, you know!"

Smirking, then trying to stifle a giggle, I watched her, trying to be serious. In that moment we were forgetting her tussle with depression, an unspoken subject – a bit like a white elephant we knew existed but never discussed. We were both behaving immaturely.

"You don't mind if I go out tonight, then?" I asked.

"No, not at all. Go and enjoy yourself. I never worry when you are with Amelia. She's a lovely, kind girl and shows a bit of common sense and can have fun."

"You really don't have to worry about me, Mum. I promise I can take care of myself. I am in the sixth form now. The world classes me as almost an adult."

"That may be, but as far as I am concerned, you are still my baby."

"Oh, honestly, Mum! I wish you wouldn't say that. It's so embarrassing."

She hugged me and kissed me delicately on the cheek. "You need to go out and enjoy yourself more. You spend far too much time studying."

"Hmm. Maybe. I'm going to do some work now before Amelia comes."

"Oh, all right. As long as you make sure you have something to eat before you go out. Now, here's the deal, I will dish your dinner up when it's ready and give you a shout."

When I was alone I disliked my own company, so when my friends weren't around, I ploughed myself into anything creative or different, to escape from my self-loathing. Art was my passion and I was good at it. In school I excelled at it. Portraits were my favourite genre. I loved the challenge of trying to catch the essence of a person on paper or canvas. People fascinated me. I was interested in what made them tick.

People-watching was a favourite pastime, assessing their clothes (fashion being my other passion), their looks and mannerisms. Superficial and meaningless, perhaps, but I wasn't interested in all that. For me it was unnecessary. I was far from meaningless; complex even. Perhaps others didn't perceive me like that, but my thoughts always seemed complicated and tormented. Why? I had no idea. And what had I to offer the world? What was my future to be? History hadn't treated me well, and my time in school was no exception. Bullying had always been a problem, especially with a certain group. Anyone unusual or different was always singled out.

As I grabbed my school folders and went up to the haven of my room, I was excited at the prospect of spending time with Amelia. I hadn't seen her in school for a few days as she had been visiting her sick nan in Devon.

I dragged myself up the stairs, each step presenting a challenge. The stairs were a killer for me but Mum liked living in the house, so I put up with them. She always maintained that going up and down stairs was good exercise for me. Gio didn't find them a handicap; she overtook me and jumped straight onto my bed. She was snuggled down on the duvet by the time I reached my room.

I could always relax and be myself in my bedroom, alone with my thoughts. Away from Mum's constant questioning and probing, as well as my sister's constant demands to borrow art stuff, books or paper. I loved my room. Mum had furnished it with ornate French ivory furniture. Its elegance pleased my aesthetic sense. The peachy walls made the room light and airy, and it always smelt fresh, clean and inviting.

When Dad's mum died a year ago, she left Mum some money. She had always felt guilty about Dad leaving us. Mum and Grandma had got on well. Dad's family had been wealthy in their time. Old money, built up from business transactions by bankers and merchants on Dad's side, dated back over 200 years. Mum was surprised to hear that she had been left £50,000 but it didn't take her long to decide what to do with it.

"Fifty grand," she said. "That will come in very handy. I can pay off my catalogues and credit card, I'll put some aside to help with uni costs for you and Izzey and I'll put a bit away for a rainy day."

The money was gone before she knew it. What she actually did was buy new furnishings for the house and then had the garden landscaped.

"I'm going to treat myself with what's left," she told me. "I might have a bit of plastic surgery and a new car."

It had made her feel really good for a time but, as always, it was short lived. I knew that money wasn't the way to solve your problems.

Hauling my school bag onto the bed, my drawings and fabrics spilled everywhere, almost covering Gio as I pulled all my work out of my portfolio. There was my design brief, sketch book containing my bodice designs, and my pattern and toile pieces. The project was to design a bodice or corset with a rococo/organic influence. So I had put together a toile made in calico, with boning and a busk, and back lacing. The main toile was complete; I was now sewing on embellishments to "flesh out" the design. Engrossed in my work, I forgot about dinner until Mum impatiently poked her head round my door.

"Your dinner's getting cold, love. I did call you."

I had been oblivious until the door opened, and Mum looked crossly at the muddle on the bed and me and Gio in the midst of it.

"Okay, I'll be right down. Sorry, Mum, I didn't hear you."

I went down to eat whilst Mum was in her room, preparing to go on her date. I could hear the hairdryer blasting, as she continued getting ready. At seven o'clock, hearing her heels clicking on the laminate floor, Mum came into the lounge with a flourish, her favourite fragrance wafting in after her.

"What do you think?" she asked, pointing with both forefingers to her cleavage in the little black number. The silky fabric of her dress clung to every curve of her body. I almost blushed, trying not to think of my mother in a compromising clinch with her potential date.

Mum was quite glamorous, despite not being well at times. Her health was never great. The bad back was due to an injury sustained as a young nurse and the side effects she suffered from the anti-depressants were linked to her two failed marriages. I secretly thought she always exaggerated things and was rather a hypochondriac.

Mum was not like me, she was considered "normal" for an adult. She had been sexy as a young woman, or so she said, and had no hang-ups about her appearance.

"Isn't that a bit OTT?" I remarked, watching her teetering on her high heels.

"No! The guys love a nice view and if he's nice as well it might help. You never know," she gushed, smiling broadly. She hurriedly fixed a pair of dangling earrings, which I privately thought did nothing to improve the look.

"Mum, dating sites are not the kind of places where you meet *nice* guys." Unable to hide my concern, I grimaced. "I wish you could meet someone from work. Surely teachers aren't snobby? Being a teaching assistant shouldn't stop them asking you out?"

"Who knows?" she replied, shrugging her shoulders. "I've given up thinking I'm going to meet someone really intelligent and nice. In any case, the teachers are all happily married, apart from one good-looking guy with an Irish accent, but I'm not good enough for *him*. Perhaps a sugar daddy will do instead?"

"I just think dating sites aren't safe. You never really know a person on the internet, do you?" My mind raced with worry, and the possible implications of these series of blind dates.

"I can look after myself, Orianna. It'll be fine."

What could I do? Let her go on her dates, if it made her feel good. At least she tried to have an interesting life. It stopped her focusing on me and my sister so much.

Izzey virtually lived at her friends' houses. She never seemed to be here, apart from when Mum was treating her to something. She was still very young and naïve.

"Can you make sure Izzey is okay? Call her mobile later?"

I nodded. "Sure." But to be honest, I didn't want to come across as the annoying big sister looking to reprimand her all the time.

Mum was concerned about her. We both knew Izzey would be okay at her mate's house, but it didn't stop Mum worrying.

❧ Two ❦

The doorbell rang as I swallowed my last mouthful of Mum's delicious roast chicken dinner.

"Are you nearly ready?" Amelia asked, when I opened the door. "The film starts at ten past eight and we have to get to Tower Park!"

"Okay, don't panic. I just need to refresh my make-up and do my hair."

"Be quick, then. I'll blame you if we miss the beginning."

Quick was something I couldn't be, especially when climbing stairs, but I hurriedly applied more mascara and lipstick and jabbed a brush at my tangled hair. I didn't always bother with make-up, but it was a confidence booster and you never knew who you were going to bump into. I looked at my reflection. Who was I kidding? What self-respecting guy was going to look twice at me, anyway?

I grabbed my coat and handbag and we headed out to Amelia's black Golf. Music from her new CD flooded the car as she turned the ignition key.

"Seat belts on, foot down, here we come!" she shouted above the music and revving of the engine as she pulled away from the kerb and entered the flow of traffic.

I had read all the books in the *Twilight* saga by Stephenie Meyer and had instantly fallen in love with Edward Cullen, the hero in the stories. His personality was just so appealing in the books – strong yet vulnerable. True love had tamed the monster within him. The paperbacks had drawn me like a magnet into their pages, spiriting me to Forks in the heart of the Olympic Peninsula in Washington State. I was totally besotted with the characters, even though none of them was real. The Cullens, Bella and Edward, were so exciting, especially Edward. I loved the way he eventually opened up to Bella once she discovered he was a vampire. He, in fact, had been more vulnerable than Bella because he had fallen in love with a human.

The soft velvet seat caressed me as the film music exploded from the surround-sound system. I was mesmerised, spellbound even. Edward and Bella were alive on the big screen in magnificent close-up. Robert Pattinson was even better in film number three than I ever imagined – sexy, sultry and perfect, and I clung to every second he was in shot. He was a fictional character, but why couldn't men like Edward actually exist? The chances of my meeting someone who could inspire in me that intensity of feeling was pure fantasy. I wished that I could just jump into the screen and be part of the film, but then, how could I compete with Bella Swan for Edward Cullen's affection...unless, of course, my blood tasted sweeter?

Sometimes I lived in a complete dream world. Mum was always complaining about me being "away with the fairies" and telling me I should try to live in the real world. How boring was that? Besides, Mum was forgetting that she had once lived in the same kind of dream world. As a teenager she loved *Grease*, *Footloose*, *Pretty in Pink* and *Mannequin* and all those crazy teen movies of the '70s and '80s. Nothing really changes.

The rustling of Amelia's popcorn in the bucket was a bit off-putting and I could even hear her crunching its contents. I wondered if she'd had any dinner; I'd never seen anything devoured that quickly. I was only halfway through my bag of pick 'n' mix when the movie finished, but then I was too immersed in the celluloid entertainment in front of me to even think about food.

As we left the cinema complex, the cold wind whipped around our shoulders, biting at our faces. It looked like the heavens were going to open yet again. Amelia guided me through the heavy glass doors and wrapped her arm tightly round mine, partly to hold me steady and partly to conserve our combined body heat.

She glanced at me, wide-eyed. "Wow, that film was amazing!"

"No!" I corrected. "Bloody amazing!"

We marched as briskly as possible towards the car park. My shoes made a dull thudding sound as they connected with the concrete paving; Amelia's heels click-clicked sexily in contrast beside me. I tried not to let it bother me.

"Wow!" Amelia exclaimed, "Edward Cullen is gorgeous! He's so protective of Bella in the film, even more than he was in the original *Twilight*."

"Yeah." I nodded in agreement, but kept my thoughts to myself.

Amelia started a conversation which echoed my own previous thoughts.

"Did you like Bella's transformation into a vampire? And Edward being so, well, gorgeous, as always, especially when he's alone with Bella?"

"Yeah, didn't you find the story spellbinding? Jacob Black was boring in comparison – apart from when he morphed into a wolf... that was pure magic. But vampires are better!"

"Guys like that just don't exist in real life, do they?" Amelia laughed in amusement.

"What, vampires? Or guys like Edward Cullen?"

"Guys like Edward Cullen." She gave an exaggerated sigh. "And if they did, they would never be interested in the likes of us."

On the way home we complained non-stop about how boring the boys at school were and how we longed for someone interesting to appear and sweep us off our feet.

When Amelia dropped me to my door, she hesitated.

"Do you want to meet up tomorrow?" she asked. "Shall we go shopping?"

Starting the weekend with a night at the movies was a great idea; continuing with shopping was even better!

"You bet. I'll pick Jess up on the way – and I'm driving – no arguments!"

"Castle Point?"

It was agreed. A girlie day out shopping in Bournemouth. What better way to lift teenage spirits?

We picked Jess up from her house. She chattered incessantly as we started the journey. At least that meant Amelia and I didn't have to try to make conversation and it made it easier for me to drive. I enjoyed driving. It was one of the few times when I felt like a normal person. Behind a steering wheel, I wasn't judged because I looked the same as everyone else. It was only when I pulled into the disabled parking bay that people reacted.

"Look at that! A carful of kids! Youth of today do just what they like!" Until they saw me get out the car, they invariably judged that I hadn't the right to park there.

I still didn't handle it very well and would pull out my blue badge and slap it on the dashboard, glancing murderously at my would-be accusers. Old people with ignorant and prejudiced attitudes really pissed me off sometimes. Jessica and Amelia found it amusing to provoke them.

"What are you staring at, Grandma?" Jessica shouted at one old lady who was glaring at us with disapproval.

The old woman turned and, leaning on her walking stick, hobbled away to avoid a confrontation.

"Did you have to do that?" I asked Jess. I felt uncomfortable at her being so confrontational. It grated on me. It looked like Amelia and I would have to curb Jessica's outspokenness today. I couldn't help worrying that one of these days she was going to overstep the mark with her insulting comments, which were uncalled for. But she continued, never really knowing when to diplomatically hold her tongue.

"Yes, actually," she raged. "Someone's got to stand up for you and it might as well be me!"

"Well, it's embarrassing and I'd rather you didn't!" I snapped. "Don't you see? I hate standing out from the crowd. It makes me feel uncomfortable."

Jess was seething. "I just think people shouldn't judge you without knowing the facts."

"That's life. You'll never change people's attitudes, Jess."

"Wanna bet?"

Amelia intervened, pushing us gently apart and breaking up our friendly dispute. "Stop it, you two! That's enough. Let's just have a nice day, without argument or confrontations, okay?"

She was right. It wasn't worth falling out over. I changed the subject and as we pranced from shop to shop, Jess filled us in with the latest school gossip, Amelia tested the newest lipsticks, staring at her reflection in the cosmetic counter mirrors and as I watched her, I just daydreamed of a time when things might be different. To be respected, perhaps have a boyfriend, eventually, and to be loved for who I was.

We were in the changing rooms of a fashion shop and into our usual subject of guys and dating.

"What's wrong with me trying to date different guys from school?" Jess wanted to know, temporarily disappearing from view under the top she was in the middle of trying on.

"It's okay to date one or two boys from school," I told her, "but not the entire sixth form. We just don't want you making a fool of yourself, that's all."

"I'm not interested in guys," Amelia said flatly, admiring the mirror image of herself in a skimpy top that left little to the imagination. "Hmm…no, I don't think that's me. I've got a few male friends from church, but they are not boyfriends," she added.

"Dating is definitely a no-no, especially with A-levels around the corner," I said. "Don't you agree, girls?"

Jess screwed her nose up and Amelia nodded in agreement. I wanted to change the subject, so that they didn't try to discuss my love life, which at this point, was non-existent.

"What do you think of this outfit, Jess?" I held up a dress on its hanger, in front of her face. "Why don't you try it on?" I urged. I was glad neither of them commented on what I tried on. Ideally, I just wanted to blend in with the background, give advice, and nothing more.

"Anything you put on looks amazing, Jess!" Amelia said.

"Yeah," I chimed in, "you could look fabulous in a bin liner!"

The day turned out to be fun. We had coffee in WH Smith and I childishly played with the froth, letting the aroma invade my nostrils. Later, after a drink and snack, we headed off, arms linked, back into the fashion shops. Clothes, hangers and arms flew around the changing room in H & M as we tried on loads of outfits. The sterile white floor of the dress shop guided me around the rails of clothes as I became fashion advisor to my friends. Jessica and Amelia came out of the changing rooms in turn while I sat in a low chair outside by the three-way mirror, trying to look interested as each of them showed me their choices.

"What do you think of this?" Amelia asked, emerging from the changing room in a long, strapless black dress.

"You look lovely, Amelia. Black really suits you, and it will go with everything for any occasion. I approve. What's it for?"

"With the parties, and proms, I thought I'd invest in something nice." Amelia grinned.

Being a student of fashion, they always picked my brains when we shopped. I liked that, though... Trinny and Susannah eat your heart out!

I encouraged Amelia to go with the black number. Jess needed no encouragement at all, and restraint was not a word she recognised. After what seemed like hours of watching them try on numerous outfits, I complimented them both generously, hoping to boost their confidence, and helped by returning their rejects to the rails.

Their energy wore me out and I envied their stamina. The whole process seemed just as long as when I went shopping with my mum and sometimes I wished the choices were much more limited – I was just glad we didn't live in London!

We headed towards Next and the shoes and accessories department at the back of the store. They both tried on very high heels, which, of course, pissed me off immediately. I knew full well just by looking at the shoes that I'd never be able to wear them. Most of the flat, ballerina styles were boring and I was fed up with wearing them, or the alternative plain loafers that did nothing for a girl's self-esteem.

I was not in the mood to shop for myself, though I did need some new outfits. I merely looked on and gave advice.

After a few hours passed, having had enough of clothes shops, I decided to head off to my favourite bookstore. It was light and airy, and I needed a break from the loud music, sweaty bodies and jam-packed rails, not to mention the oh-so-smiley shop assistants.

"Girls, I'm going to head for the bookshop, while you queue to pay. Is that okay? I know you'll be in here for ages yet."

Peering through the huge floor-to-ceiling windows of Waterstones, I scanned the promotions before going inside to see what else was on offer. The usual authors' works were there, J K Rowling, Stephenie Meyer, Kristin Cast and P C Cast, Philippa Gregory and, of course, the Penguin classics.

In the fashion section, I stumbled across a copy of *9 Heads: A Guide to Drawing Fashion* by Nancy Riegelman. Turning over the pink and white cover, I slouched into one of the deep bucket seats that were strategically dotted around the store, and flicked through the different fashion illustrations. Looking for inspiration, I had found a huge page-turner, heaped with step-by-step ideas on fashion illustration, colour photographs and ideas for putting together presentation boards – exactly what I was looking for.

Looking around me for a moment, I felt a twinge of hope that I would bump into a cute, intelligent guy in the non-fiction section, just like movie characters did. Hopelessly romantic, I knew that such a scenario would never include the likes of me. Outside, the pavement was packed with people; mothers pulling their screaming kids along, grumpy husbands who wanted to go home and watch the football, and young women giggling and chattering as they struggled to carry their many purchases. The media told us daily that we were in a recession; there was a "credit crunch". Watching all this retail therapy made me seriously question that.

I was in a quiet haven, glued to my seat, thumbing through my potential purchase, when I happened to look up and spot an incredible-looking guy, who had just entered the store. He also was looking through the books on art and design. The thing about him that I just couldn't ignore were his amazing blue eyes; they reminded me of miniature swimming pools. He didn't notice me, but then I was unnoticeable…I was sitting down. Thank God I was, I thought. At least he couldn't judge me; I looked like any "normal" person perusing a book.

I peered at him through my lowered lashes, watching and hoping that he wouldn't meet my gaze. My eyes flickered back and forth between him and the book I was strategically nursing.

He queued at the till to make his purchase. From my vantage point, he looked about my age, 17, maybe even 18 at most. As I watched, enjoying the view, he walked out of the shop, carrier bag in hand, and then disappeared from view.

My arms ached and my fingers were numb and red, weighted down by my friends' carrier bags from nearly every shop. It wasn't even my shopping. They had bought so much that neither of them could carry their purchases by themselves. I'd been good. My only purchase had been one book from Waterstones to help me with my course. Amelia and Jess fell in a heap, bags and all, as they squeezed into the car for home.

"You're very quiet. Are you okay?" Jess asked.

"Yes, thanks. I'm just a bit tired. I will be okay later, once I get home and rest. You know, it's the walking, and the pain I'm in gets me down."

"Sometimes you are so in your own world, we never know if we might have upset you," Amelia questioned.

"Not at all," I replied, as I collapsed into the driving seat, starting the engine. Heading for the car park exit, I followed the familiar signs, focusing on the road ahead that led home.

Jess pulled her purchases out onto her lap appraising them again, whilst chatting to her mum on her mobile, relaying how much money she'd spent and exactly what she'd bought. Meanwhile, Amelia sang along to the latest chart music which belted out from the radio...her way of avoiding Jess's constant prattle.

Home alone, I later crashed out on the sofa and caught up with a couple of soap operas I had recorded on Sky Plus, before heating a small pizza and taking myself off to bed for an early night. Mum was dating again, so I knew she wouldn't be in until the early hours. I snuggled into my pillows with my hardback copy of *Twilight* and a packet of chocolate biscuits. I knew I'd spend tomorrow finishing coursework, waiting for Mum to surface from her bed, if she ever came back home from her date at all and possibly argue with Iz about what programmes to watch on TV. So, just another boring weekend; no different from any other almost over with.

❧ Three ❦

School was not a place to meet a hero like Edward Cullen, I pondered, as I drove to the student car park. Life was tedious! The same old routine … copious amounts of work to do in the day, followed by heaps of homework at night. I desperately wanted to get my art qualifications, to get my portfolio together for my college interviews and escape from here. The only people to give me some light relief were Amelia, Jack and Jess, and together we were a strange mix.

Wimborne Upper School was small in comparison to others in the area, having only 900 registered students, including sixth form. All the students had grown up together, which was why everyone knew everyone intimately. It was a close-knit community. For me that didn't matter, as I never felt I fully fitted in anywhere. Physically, I knew I never would fit in. I didn't relate that well to people, especially people I didn't know. At this point, I was closer to my mum than anyone else on earth, but I was never truly in harmony with her. We didn't always have the same opinions on everything. The only person I agreed with a lot of the time was Amelia and today we would catch up on things, as it was just another day at school. Or so I thought.

I pulled up in the car park next to Amelia's VW. I had loads to carry; my portfolio and all my fashion work. The air felt fresh and cool against my skin, even though my woollen coat was pulled snugly around me. In my usual clumsy fashion, I walked towards the red-brick school building, stumbling, as my feet almost collapsed beneath me. A jolting muscle spasm pulsed through my body as I found the deep pothole and almost went flying. Bloody legs! I definitely needed a new body. I felt the heat in my cheeks as my face flushed scarlet, realising that my ungainliness had attracted an audience. A tall figure was leaning against the driver's door of an expensive-looking car, staring intently in my direction. I could feel his eyes boring into me as his gaze continued to follow me. I tried to look away, but he was very good looking and hard to ignore. Was he new? I wondered how I hadn't noticed this guy at school before. He was staring at me now; didn't he know it was rude to stare?

How ignorant! I complained to myself. Typical bloke, they had no idea how to behave until they were at least 30. Why didn't he ask me if I wanted any help? Anyway, who needed a guy, no matter how good looking he was? And boy, was he good looking! He stood about 6ft 2in with dark brown hair and he had the most piercing blue eyes.

Hang on, hadn't I seen him before? He was the guy from the bookstore the other day! I'd never forget those eyes. He certainly wasn't flashy in a vulgar way, but smart and clean-cut in his designer casuals. His clothes looked expensive, and his car certainly was. It was a sleek, black Audi R8. I remembered watching the TV programme *Top Gear* and Jeremy Clarkson had rated the car 17/20 for coolness. But what stuck in my mind was the price – they ranged between £71,000 and £81,000. Phew! This guy was no Mr Ordinary.

Trying to ignore his gaze, I gave him one more glance and then regretted it. He continued to glare in my direction; his cobalt eyes full of revulsion. Why? He didn't know me. What had I done wrong? I was embarrassed as I passed him and tried to melt into the gathering groups of students. The catchphrase "you look like the back end of a bus" suddenly ran through my mind and I waddled with more haste than usual, trying to concentrate more decidedly now with every step, into the building.

Finally, I reached registration, still flushed from the process of carrying all my worldly shackles and encountering that new boy. Piling my stuff up in front of me on the table, I collapsed into the unfriendly, plastic grey chair in silence.

Amelia looked at me with concern and leaned in closer to me. "What's the matter, Orianna? Are you okay?"

"I'm okay! I just nearly went head over heels into a pothole in the car park with all my stuff nearly flying everywhere, but I'm all right."

She didn't quite believe me. "And?"

"And what?" Sometimes her probing annoyed me.

"There's something else bothering you, isn't there? I know that face!"

Amelia wore that irritating smug look of hers. She was a caring girl but didn't always come across that way. She could sometimes be pretty abrupt. All her family were evangelical Christians, which didn't bother me because I, too, had a faith and a relationship with God; I just wasn't too vocal about it. Amelia's interests were similar to mine. She liked design, fashion, music, reading novels and going to the cinema. I considered her to be a good friend and confidante as she had a maturity beyond her years and was sensible, but could also be good fun to be with. Her mother spoilt her rotten, especially when she did well at school. Our group of like-minded friends stuck together, by ourselves, away from the usual cliques of girls who always seemed to know everyone else's business.

"Oh, I just saw this guy in the car park," I said, I hoped with nonchalance. "He's new, I think. Well, you would remember him if you'd seen him before. He was staring, and really rude."

"What do you mean, staring and rude?" Amelia was intrigued now, hoping to get the full story. She moved her chair closer to mine.

"Well, when I stumbled, he just stared at me. Never said a word, just kept on staring. It was weird and he never even offered to help. Never spoke, just stared."

My face was obviously betraying my feelings. So much so that Amelia continued to question me.

"Who was he? What did he look like? Anyone we know?"

I began to wish I'd kept my mouth shut. "Well, I don't know him. He was tall, with dark brown hair and *really* blue eyes, and he was standing next to this expensive car, a black Audi—"

"R8!" Jack butted in behind us, forcing himself into the conversation. "That's Ashley Mason. His dad's really rich, a plastic surgeon or something, I think. He's with the IT crowd."

I hadn't realised we had been speaking loud enough to be overheard.

Amelia's eyes lit up with excitement. "He sounds interesting—"

Jack again butted in, cutting her off mid-sentence. "Don't think of trying to date him, girls." He grinned. "You'll be lucky. According to most of the girls here, he doesn't date. They all think he's gorgeous, of course, but don't waste your time, Orianna. He *definitely* doesn't date. Apparently none of the girls here are rich or good looking enough for him," he continued, almost smugly. "He's shallow and only interested in what you look like on the outside. Believe you me, Orianna, I don't mean to be cruel, but he wouldn't like your waddle. Pretty girls are a status symbol to him, much like his car!"

Jack's comments didn't surprise me in the least. Jack, I knew, would like to be the most fanciable guy in school, but it was so obvious from his over-friendly, sometimes pushy demeanour, that his wish would never be granted. Jack wasn't the least bit like the tortured soul of Heathcliff in *Wuthering Heights* or Mr Darcy in *Pride and Prejudice*.

Jack was the next in line in my motley crew. He was fun and very lively, with a dry sense of humour. He would crack jokes, but the girls never understood them. He loved comedians like Eddie Izzard and Lee Evans and was always trying to be at the centre of attention or the conversation. Jack Stephens could draw... boy, could he draw. He was one of the best in our school at art. Art lessons with him were a real hoot! He loved flirting with girls. Any girls.

The teacher taking the register glared over the top of her glasses at us, punching the keys on the keyboard. We were talking too much. I thought we should be talking about something more important than Ashley Mason. He was a jerk. I vividly remembered the deep blue of his eyes as he'd glared at me this morning. He was certainly no gentleman! Bloody black Audi R8 owner! Perhaps he was repulsed by my disability. It was the only possible conclusion I could come to. The thought of it made my blood boil. I was just the same as everyone else, with the same emotions and feelings, the same desires and needs. From now on, I decided, if I came across him, I would avoid him at all costs. If he wasn't prepared to look past my disability, then he wasn't worth knowing!

"Hell-o-o?"

I realised I had been completely in a daydream when Jack's voice brought me back to reality.

"Sorry... what?" I asked.

"Don't waste your time worrying about him," Jack retorted, his own, more familiar, blue eyes blazing with jealousy. "Life isn't a fairytale, you know. He won't whisk you away on his white charger, or even in his flash Audi R8!"

"Hasn't anyone ever told you, Jack? Life isn't fair!" I snapped at him, hoping to end the conversation. I knew he wasn't meaning to be horrible, just realistic, in his usual cynical way. He meant well. He just bluntly stated the obvious at times.

"You could always have me!" he joked, but deep down I knew Jack wasn't joking, he was serious. This certainly wasn't the way I wanted our friendship to go. I sighed to myself in despair, not quite knowing how to reply. Jack was staring now, waiting to see my reaction, but I thought it best to ignore the comment, as if I had never heard him say it.

Seconds later, the end of registration bell rang and Amelia and I were saved from Jack trying to flirt and be nice to us. Textiles, more textiles, then later we had art. Bliss … a chance to relax and concentrate all at the same time. I hoped that throwing myself into my work would make me forget about the unsettling encounter with that guy in the car park earlier.

The first few periods went very well; I caught up with all my work in textiles, and Mrs Mulvihill was really pleased with my work. I fitted the bodice and skirt onto the dummy, and Mrs Mulvihill checked all the detail and embroidery.

"This is wonderful, Orianna, absolutely exquisite work," she said proudly. "There isn't any way you could improve it – I think you will get a distinction for it." She was gushing at me like I was her favourite student or something. It was embarrassing with the other students looking on. I didn't want to be a teacher's pet; I'd much rather get a better mark. But that's how she was – very bubbly, and always positive and complimentary and I loved her lessons because she was such an inspiration to me. She knew all there was to know about the fashion industry, and was always trying to get us to work with industrial methods of sewing, producing items with a professional finish. She said it would help us prepare for degree-level work, if that was the direction we chose to go in.

When the lunch bell rang, I grabbed my bag, realising my stomach was growling, and started to make my way to the lunch hall. It was no surprise to hear Jack yelling after me.

"Anna! Wait up! I'll walk with you to lunch." I slowed my steps until he was walking beside me in his habitual place of loyal friend. We queued in the line with our trays, choosing what we wanted to eat. I had the healthy option and Jack chose the opposite. We usually sat in the far corner of the school cafeteria at lunchtime. This was our normal spot, so that if Amelia and Jess couldn't find us, they would know where to look. The thought of having to sit near the "it" crowd always made me and Amelia cringe.

I stared at the boring posters on the wall, while Jess took out her compact and checked her make-up, constantly flicking her blonde hair extensions as she filled Jack in on the latest gossip about who was going out with whom, and who had broken up with whom. Their small talk bored me rigid and I desperately wanted something new to happen.

Amelia came over and surreptitiously joined in the conversation, trying to gain Jack's attention. I flicked through the book on the artist Euan Uglow, whose work I had been studying for some time. Very methodical in his approach, and measured, his paintings were clean, crisp and clear cut. I hoped some day to work like him. My work was too "fluffy" in comparison, too impressionistic.

I drowned out the inane chatter by burying myself in my book until the bell rang, stirring me from my daydream. Lunch was over. I put my books in my bag and went off to afternoon registration, and then art. I didn't want to talk to anyone. I was not in the mood.

Art was a breeze for Jack and he was flirting with the girls, as usual, as we started to get our work set up for the lesson. They were used to him and largely ignored his remarks, so he gave up and came to work beside me.

"Hey, hon…you okay?" he asked. "You were quiet at lunch. Anything up?"

"No, not at all. Just engrossed in some art books, trying to get some inspiration." I didn't want to tell him that I had been contemplating my unusual encounter with Ashley Mason. I still couldn't fathom him out.

I had begun working on a series of self-portraits on canvas. It didn't mean I was self-absorbed; it was just a form of expressing the different facets of my personality. I was working with acrylics, but preferred oils. Acrylics could be quite flat looking, but the school had a limited budget, so acrylics it had to be. My paintings were coming on well; I was working one canvas as a tonal, in shades of blue, another was monochrome and the last, full colour. The last one was working out the best.

Our art teacher put the register away and came over to critique my work.

"Hi, Orianna, that is working well today. Those colours are blending fantastically. Hmm, a very impressionistic statement, with good use of light and colour."

Mr Ridgeway was not normally very vocal in his appraisal of students' work. His normal stance was to peer over your shoulder, stare at your work, half-smile if it was good and then move away. He seemed to be one of those deep and silent types. Most of the sixth form girls fancied him, but we all knew he was married. In any case, he was far too old for us; he must have been at least 35! In previous lessons, we had watched him do some portrait work. His sketching was incredible and the likenesses he produced were so accurate. He was a complete inspiration.

I tried to concentrate. My mood lightened a little, I giggled to myself as I heard Jack flirting again, as he wandered around the studio, brush in hand.

"So, Joanna, what colour undies are you wearing today? Would you like me to paint a portrait of you in them? You could be Rose in *Titanic* posing for Jack?"

"No! I don't think so!" She tried not to show a slight trace of laughter, she didn't want Jack to realise she enjoyed his attentions.

"Oh, go on! Please? I need to improve my portrait painting and you are ideal subject matter." From his expression it was almost as if he was imagining the sight of Jo in virtually nothing. My shoulders shuddered as I cringed; sometimes he overstepped the mark.

"Only because you want to see me in my lace underwear, Jack, you naughty boy."

Joanne grinned at him. All the girls teased him so, but he did ask for it. Jack was always having in-depth conversations with the girls in the class, about the style and colour of their underwear. His next favourite subject was being in a band; who would be his roadies, groupies and his eventual wife. When he wasn't incessantly chatting, he'd plug into his iPod, discreetly trying to listen to his downloaded tunes, without being noticed. It would be his own fault if he got the bloody thing confiscated, which was what happened if teachers caught you with mobiles or iPods. Mind you, Jack liked to break the rules and try to get away with it. I suppose that was his way of trying to be like the "it" crowd, without actually being in it.

There were no takers from the girls for posing for Jack. It was obvious no one would do it, but the conversations did make us all laugh. Art was never dull with Jack. His Dorset accent could be heard a few decibels above everyone else. He could be lazy, and hardly ever put himself wholeheartedly into his work. He didn't need to; he was so talented. However, he was not as good as one other person whose work I had just begun to see lying around the studio. It belonged to a student whose name seemed to be springing up everywhere in conversation and sadly in my memory - Ashley Mason! It was weird, but ever since I'd encountered him, people were mentioning his name all the time. It was starting to grate on me..

I carried on with my work, deep in thought, contemplating the brush strokes I was making, when I suddenly realised someone was standing right behind me.

"That's really rather good," a velvety voice said, over my shoulder.

I was reminded of smooth, dark chocolate that slowly melts on the tongue. Smooth or not, I almost jumped out of my skin because someone was addressing *me*! Turning around on the balls of my feet, trying to keep my balance, I was stunned as I realised I was staring straight into Ashley Mason's piercing blue eyes. In my surprised state, I could feel my face turning pink. I had to look down to reassemble my tangled thoughts.

He smiled at me briefly, almost as if he was trying to suppress a grin and then transferred his gaze to my canvas. "The likeness is very good; portraits are your genre, aren't they?" He looked wistful as he spoke.

I don't know what surprised me most, his positive comments, or the rather posh accent in which he expressed them.

"I'm not as good at portraits as I am at landscapes and graphic work," he continued, decidedly, giving me another smile. Folding his arms, he looked contemplative for a moment, looking at my portrait. The day was becoming decidedly strange. His smile could melt butter! Now I could see what all the fuss was about…why half the girls in school, I had heard, wanted to date him. He was talented, artistic, good-looking and rich, with good manners. Although I had initially thought him rude, he seemed charming, polite, determined, and possibly over confident. To me he was impossibly beautiful; almost perfect His facial features could have been sculpted…angular high cheekbones, strong jawline, a straight nose, and full lips. Almost too perfect; a model type. His hairstyle, seemingly always messy and unkempt, was designed to look that way – sexy, unruly, as if he'd just come from his bed. And those eyes…bolts of electric blue that pierced the very soul.

As he walked away from me, I noticed his slender, but muscular body through his shirt. What a package! But for me, there was still one problem, his attitude towards me. It was ridiculous that I should be so elated because Ashley Mason knew my name. Even so, in the days that followed I caught myself daydreaming about him, and Amelia and Jack would pass their hands across my eyes, "Hel-lo?" "You in there, Anna?"

I couldn't stop thinking about him; I even doodled his name on a piece of paper and stared at it as I worked. It seemed to bring him close in some strange way. I wondered if he felt like that about me. Huh, who was I kidding?

❧ Four ❧

Another week or so had passed. We were well into the routine of school. Our freetime was in a routine rut. Amelia, Jess and I sat with Jack in his lounge. Everything was ticking over as normal – Mum's dates and disasters, shopping, and Amelia and I chatting and social networking.

Amelia gasped and I stared open-mouthed at the images on Jack's laptop. We were both completely shocked to see Aimee Anson's Facebook profile and photos. They were disgusting; she and her mates posing as if they were glamour models, scantily clad, with their boobs spilling out. There were other photos, including some of her and Nathan mauling each other next to a heap of empty lager cans, with their mates smoking in the background. It looked like they were all hanging out in a local park in the middle of the night. Amelia and I clocked the pictures and just looked at each other in disbelief. At that moment, I decided to turn the laptop off. I couldn't look at them any more. They were bringing themselves and their families into disrepute and weren't doing school any favours, either.

Jack carried on flirting with Jess. He wasn't taking any notice of what we were viewing on his laptop. At that moment he was being silly and crying at *Quadrophenia*. Jack's fashion style was late '70s–early '80s, much like the style of the house. Memorabilia of the era was everywhere. His parents lived in a time-warp, which clearly influenced Jack, giving him a certain quirkiness. It was funny.

His parents, James and Mary Stephens worked in the local supermarket. They had met at the height of the "Mods and Rockers" cult when Vespa riding groups of Mods would head to the coasts, particularly at bank holiday weekends, clashing with the Rockers on their powerful motorbikes. Jack had a scooter. At this precise moment, it was lying in bits on their back lawn.

"Do you actually know what you are doing with that, Jack?" I'd said to him when he'd taken us out there to see it.

He'd laughed. "Yeah, course I do, Marilyn!"

"Why does he call you that?" Jess wanted to know.

"My eyebrows are like hers… oh, and because of my famous wiggle!" We'd all laughed at that, except Jess.

"You shouldn't let him take the piss, Anna. It's not funny!"

"We are only having fun. Don't be so serious!" If I couldn't take the mickey out of myself, then who could?

"You look nothing like Marilyn!" Jess said.

GOD… wasn't that the point…?

Jack's pet hates were plastic-looking, self-important girls in the style of Jordan or Jodie Marsh, or something off of *The Only Way is Essex*, the kind of girls who thought only their looks mattered. Jess was not his cup of tea. She was quite petite with very blonde highlighted hair and badly applied hair extensions. She had small blue eyes and a round, dainty face. No one could forget her birthday. About a week before 4th August, she announced it like a foghorn, to get as much attention as possible. She loved and craved attention from guys; one of her pet aspirations was to go out with fit guys who were out of her league. She was always hankering after Nathan Cooper, but he was never interested. Having fun and hanging out with friends were what she lived for. The two things that irritated me the most were the way she always wore a gel bra in the hope it would attract the advances of boys, and her habit of constantly flicking back her hair with her hand like an outdated *Big Brother* contestant who had outstayed her welcome.

Jess was a nice enough friend and would do anything for me, but we were just on completely different wavelengths. So, along with her constant chattering about who was dating who, sometimes she could be a bit much. She tried to talk in American slang all the time, to hide her Dorset accent. It amused me that she hated girls who were false, even though she could be at times. She loved romantic movies and always cried at them. Her style was hot fashion, but "cheap and cheerful" styles like River Island, Primark and Top Shop.

The only thing I didn't like about Jack was that he smoked, as did Jessica. It was nerdy now, and so bad for you. Amelia and I sat there wreathed in clouds of smoke, tea drinking, laughing and generally teasing Jack. Just a normal day at Jack's house. Not that I felt like my friends. Far from it. All I could do was daydream about Ashley. Perhaps I was becoming obsessed? That would be it…I had developed another problem, AMOD, or Ashley Mason Obsessive Disorder. I was so glad that none of my friends had noticed…yet!

I was lying casually on a picnic blanket, on a hillside, in a remote part of the idyllic countryside not too far from Gold Hill, one of the highest points in Dorset. As I stared into the distance, the summer sun wrapped my whole being in its warmth. Swallows swooped and circled above me, gathering tiny insects to feed to their young, and I was aware of a blackbird trilling merrily on an elder branch. Further down the hill a farmer was mowing a hayfield, chugging slowly up and down on his tractor. Bees buzzed around lazily, foraging deeply into the foxgloves. The sounds of summer were all too apparent. I felt happy, relaxed and elated.

I became aware of a figure, sitting cross-legged beside me, staring intently at me with pencil and sketchbook in hand. Was this person drawing me? I turned to get a better look. It was Ashley Mason.

How strange. I hadn't arranged to meet him like this, especially not alone, nor to do with art. He, too, looked relaxed and comfortable. His white linen shirt hung loosely around him, exposing his chest where it was unbuttoned.

"What are we doing here?" I asked.

He looked up, giving me a slow, twinkly smile. "You wanted me to draw you."

As he sketched, his movements with the pencil were strong and confident. He said he felt alive when drawing; he loved the experience of trying to capture the spirit of a person at a particular moment in time. I knew exactly what he meant; it was like probing a person's soul. There was something special about this place with him sitting there. I wasn't exactly sure what I was meant to be feeling.

"Maybe I did, but I can't remember…"

Suddenly, a piercing din broke into the scene of calm. For a moment I wondered what was going on, until I awoke to the loud and urgent ringing of my bedside alarm clock. Blast! I had been dreaming. Rubbing my eyes, I pushed back my bed-tousled hair. Damn the bloody clock; why did it have to wake me up?

Part of me felt that last night's dream was real and it was really difficult to argue with that. I had smelt the freshly mown hay, and Ashley's aftershave. I had felt the soft breeze stroking my face. I tried to remember parts of the dream, as if keeping them locked in my imagination would somehow bring them to life.

I didn't remember asking him to meet me for an art lesson! I was aware of my heart thudding rapidly in my chest, recalling this dream. How bad was that? I must be really obsessed to be dreaming about him. Reluctantly, I pulled myself up in bed. The clock, silent now, indicated that it was time to get up and get ready for school.

Earthly, human activities claimed my dream space as I showered and dressed and did my hair and make up. With eyeliner, mascara, a touch of blusher and pink lipstick, I created the mask I showed to the world. Trundling down the stairs, I remembered Mum had been out on dates all week. I had to ask her how they went.

Mum flitted around the kitchen, making tea.

"Want one?" she asked in her usual subdued morning tone. Mum needed several cups of tea before she could function, and having a full-blown, in-depth conversation was out of the question.

"Mmm, thanks, Mum. How were your dates, by the way?"

She sighed and slouched her shoulders. "The same as usual. The men on those sites are all the same, just after one thing. Oh, don't look so worried, Anna, I didn't give in!"

I felt relieved inside. What was the matter with these men that they couldn't see the amazing person that she was?

"I'm glad to hear it. That's not the way to get a guy, by just jumping into bed with him! Okay, okay...I know you are not like that. Just wait until the right one comes along." The last thing I wanted to do was lecture her. I had no experience of these matters but I knew she was worth a hell of a lot more than a quick shag.

"How was school yesterday?" She obviously wanted to change the subject.

"Not bad." I couldn't really think of anything else to say. School had been pretty uneventful up until Ashley had introduced himself. However, I was not going to let Mum know anything and in any case, there was nothing to say. I sat down at the kitchen table, buttering the freshly popped toast. Mum plonked a mug of hot tea down in front of me, which I relished. The first cup of the day was always the best.

She gave a little shake of her head. "We never seem to get time to talk, do we? How's your love life, anyway? It has to be better than mine, a good looking girl like you!"

Taking a bite from my toast, I cleared my throat in response. "For goodness' sake, Mum! Get real. No one is going to be interested in me. Guys want a perfect physical package. Most of them are so shallow, personality doesn't even figure in the equation." I tried not to raise my voice at her, but surely she knew by now how uncomfortable I was talking about this subject? I continued to munch on my toast, in the hope that if I had a mouthful of breakfast I wouldn't be required to speak.

"So you think the way you are will stop you getting a decent boyfriend, do you?" she growled, before swigging her tea down in three great gulps.

I shrugged my shoulders at her in annoyance. "*Any* boyfriend! Now let's change the subject, shall we?" I wriggled uncomfortably. I couldn't see *anyone* being interested in me in *that* way. Sure, Jack was interested but we were so far gone as friends now, that anything else would seem almost incestuous. I sometimes wondered if able-bodied people actually ever thought about what it was like to have a disability – or did they just never think about it unless it actually happened to them?

Not that I dwell on having a disability; I'm not obsessive about it. I've had to learn to live with it, regardless. I do wonder sometimes why God chose me to have this. Is that the wrong way of thinking? Sometimes, my warped mind wondered whether I'd been given this disability to eventually be healed, so that it would prove God's glory. Lost it, or what? Hell, who knew what God's plans were? I certainly didn't feel I figured in them.

All this talk of boys was making me cross and uncomfortable. Mum always managed to embarrass me by pointing out my faults and failings, even though she was, in her own mind, being kind. Because she was over protective as well as critical, I shied away from her closeness, fiercely defending my independence. In that sense, I guess my attitude was as normal as any other teenager's. Would that change as I grew older? I hoped so.

I sipped the hot, strong tea. "Mum, do we really have to talk about boys?" I continued munching on my toast until I had finished it.

She shrugged, mercifully changing the subject. "Did you get all your homework done?"

"Yes, it's all under control. I'm handing it in today." I put my cup down on the table and pecked her quickly on the lips.

"Have a good day," I called out, grabbing my school bag and heading out. "Bye!"

Fifteen minutes later, I pulled up in the student car park. I realised I had parked alongside the black Audi R8, and wished I had parked in another space, but before I could move elsewhere, I saw Ashley getting out of his car. I blushed as he gave me a cheeky smile. My heart fluttered, and I was embarrassed by the blushing, but with him around it was inevitable. I wondered if he had any idea of the effect this had on the girls around him. He surely wasn't oblivious to it?

He moved towards my car and the fluttering turned to racing; he wasn't even close to me. Then he saw his friends were watching him. They called to him from the other side of the car park, so he quickly changed direction and walked off towards them.

Perhaps he was rude, after all. Maybe his kind comments were just that – comments, and I was reading much more into them. Stupid idiot! Too gullible by half. I knew I would never learn and would end up getting into trouble one day.

As Ashley walked off, I noticed him take a sneaking glance back in my direction, and then I saw Nathan Cooper elbow him disapprovingly. I disliked that boy; he was arrogant, self-obsessed and ignorant. I couldn't begin to imagine why Ashley was friendly with Nathan as they didn't seem to have anything in common. They were entirely different. Both their families had money; maybe that was the connection – that, and their propensity for wearing designer clothes.

Anyway, I had to forget about them. With Ashley it was hard though; I could see in him qualities that set him apart from everyone else. Not rudeness, as I had first thought, but sensitivity, kindness, and a sense of fun.

I sensed there were also some deeper attributes. He seemed more thoughtful and caring. Yes, definitely hidden depths, and I longed to get to know him, but it was virtually impossible with his friends around. They were so different from Jack, Amelia and Jess. The "it" crowd moved in different circles, both in and out of school, so the likelihood of there ever being any connection between me and Ashley was remote.

"How did your mum get on with her dates?" Amelia asked during registration. I didn't really want to talk about potential romances, least of all my mother's.

"As usual," I replied, pulling a face. "Total waste of time and effort." I hoped Amelia would change the subject, but she didn't.

"But she is so nice. I have no idea why she can't find a good man. Do you think it is those online dating sites?"

"Probably. I've told her most of the men on there are just after sex or are scammers from Nigeria; and Mum is worth more than that."

"Yeah, you're right. I love your mum, she could do so much better." Amelia's hand found my shoulder. "What about you, then? When are you going to find yourself a nice fella? Most sixth formers have serious relationships now, isn't it about time we found someone for you?"

This was exactly why I wanted to discontinue the conversation and had tried to be abrupt, but it obviously wasn't working.

Jack was busy earwigging as usual, and butted in.

"I'd take you out on a date. What do you think?" he said, looking straight at me.

I could feel myself blushing for the second time since I entered the school gates. I knew Amelia had a soft spot for him, so I tried to play it cool. She was glaring at Jack. I felt sorry for Amelia as Jack was behaving more and more like my faithful puppy dog, and it was becoming difficult to shake him off.

"Jack, you know it would never work between us, we have been friends for too long, and we know each other too well," I said, diplomatically.

"Oh well, you can't blame me for trying!" he chirped playfully, but his expression told me that he wasn't feeling this flippant inside. I closed my eyes, sighing to myself in frustration.

"Who do you like, Orianna?" Amelia asked. She looked pleased that I'd snubbed Jack and now had no idea what my answer might be.

"That would be telling!" I joked. "If I liked someone, do you seriously think I would tell you guys? You'd be trying to get me fixed up in no time!"

"Well? Is that such a bad thing?" Amelia was beaming now, hoping that I would perhaps reveal who I was interested in, so that she could make her move and set us up; anything to get Jack to lose interest in me. I knew this was her motive; her face was so readable and I had known her for too long to not know what she was thinking.

"Anna, can we talk later? I really need to speak with you, just us. Is that O.K?"

"Yes, Amelia! Now let's drop the subject, please." I didn't give anything away, making sure my expression revealed nothing.

Registration was over, and to avoid any more talk of dating, I headed off in a hurry to my first lesson, which was art. I set up my canvasses and development work and began working on my paintings again. I had to get them finished and they had to be right. Mr Ridgeway, the art teacher, was his usual laid-back self and always an inspiration. We had all morning with him, so I was going to relax and enjoy the day.

My legs were painful and troublesome, but it didn't matter when I was painting. I would escape into my own dream world as usual, and enjoy being me.

My emotional calm was blown suddenly when Ashley came into the studio and began to set up his easel next to mine. My heart began to pound in my chest. God, could anyone else hear its rhythmic thumping?

What was wrong with me? He was only a guy! I could see him looking at me as he set up his work. His lips formed a very sensual smile and his eyes twinkled as he spoke.

"Hello there. My name's Ashley, Ashley Mason. I'm so sorry I've never introduced myself properly before." His voice met the air like silk flowing sensually over my skin.

"Hi. I heard that's what your name was. How are you?" I asked. I was really trying not to give away any emotion.

"Very good, thank you." He raised an eyebrow. "I hope you have only heard good things about me?" His mellow voice permeated my brain and his gaze linked with mine. I hadn't realised just how deep blue his eyes were. They looked almost unnatural, a deep cobalt blue. I would have sworn he wore contacts, but I wasn't close enough to tell. He looked amazing and his style suited him. Although designer clothes were obvious, he never actually looked over dressed. His fashion sense seemed to be perfect.

He was wearing a navy blue silk shirt, with the sleeves rolled back, over a Gap t-shirt in dark grey, with dark grey trousers. Being interested in fashion, I liked his style.

He stood beside me, perfect in every way. His skin was flawless, the blue eyes sparkled wickedly and he was flirtatious. He propped up a mirror beside him on the workbench, and proceeded to examine his profile as he stood in front of the easel. Taking a freshly sharpened pencil from his bag, he began to draw, studying himself intently in the mirror. I watched in awe as his pencil danced over the canvas.

"To be honest," I said, "I only knew what your name was from hearing people talk in tutor time, that's all. The boys discuss your car, and wonder how you can afford it." I had to admit I was intrigued by that, too.

I continued working on my full-colour self-portrait, wondering whether that would be the entirety of our conversation or not. Instead of working from life, I was using a recent photograph Amelia had taken during the summer holidays. I was happy with how the painting was working out, but his presence beside me was distracting. I pretended not to be interested, but could not help peeping now and again. It was spellbinding. We exchanged a few meaningful glances, but there was no conversation between us.

When our eyes did meet, he didn't look quite as aloof as he had previously. He looked at me curiously, as if trying to weigh me up. He didn't seem to realise how talented he was and that just made me fancy him more than ever. I would have to keep it to myself. Not even my friends must know. I couldn't bear the rejection if he wasn't interested.

Surely he must have a girlfriend? Why on earth would he not have? It was not my place to ask him, so how would I find out? Should I push the conversation further with him? Was it too forward of me, when we didn't really know each other? Maybe I could try.

To break the ice a bit more, I thought I would pay him a compliment and see what happened.

"So…do you like your painting?" I asked, feeling awkward and stupid as I spoke. My heart started to thump in my chest as I realised I could potentially be making a complete fool of myself.

He laughed. The sound was soft and enchanting. He gave me a crooked smile that sent my disordered knees to jelly. I could only stare back at him like an idiot.

The smile began to fade away. He was obviously wondering if I was mentally deranged.

"It's not too bad, but there are faults with it. It needs working on to show my identity more."

I was showing off, just a little bit. I knew that my portrait work was superior…spectacular even. I may have been a failure in terms of physical action or beauty, but I could paint a mean portrait. His own admission of this was apparent in his manner and tone of voice as he compared his work to mine. His eyes flickered from my work to his own canvas.

"How come I have never seen you before?" I asked, changing the subject.

"I am relatively new here," he replied as he continued to work. "My dad is a plastic surgeon and was working in London, but he wanted to live in the countryside, so we moved to Witchampton. I was at a private school but I hated it and wanted to experience the same kind of education as the average teenager and not be treated differently just because my dad's in the high-income bracket." He spoke with such self-assurance – he really acted older than his age.

"Oh, I see. Now I know why your accent is different and you drive the car you do!"

He frowned. "Look, please don't misunderstand the situation. I am not 'up myself' or materialistic, if that is what you think? It's just that my dad wanted his kids to have equal, if not better opportunities in life. He likes to mix in different social circles, as he reckons it gives us a greater understanding of people and life. That's why he agreed to let me finish off my education here, so that I would not become blinkered and single-minded, as a lot of people with money can be."

Well, that was me told! But I was impressed with what he had to say. "That's a good philosophy to have. I like the sound of your dad, he seems very down to earth." So Ashley was not as I perceived him to be at all, and that was a refreshing surprise.

"Well, he went into plastic surgery not just to titivate and massage the egos of middle- and upper-class women, by enhancing their breasts or giving them cute nose-jobs, but also to work with the disfigured. Plastic surgery is important and helps them rebuild their lives and return to normality after a car crash, or fire, for instance."

I could tell he was trying not to sound pompous or patronising. In fact, he seemed to be the total opposite to all the friends he hung out with.

"Your dad sounds very noble. Are you much alike?" I wanted to hear his answer. I always hoped if people had met my mum they would say we were not too much alike. I wanted to be an individual, with my own aspirations and ideas.

"Yes, I think so, in some ways. We have the same characteristics, the same way of looking at things. We get on well."

"That's great!" I said, not knowing what to say next and hoping I was not giving away the effect he was having on me. It was nice for him that he was close to his dad; I wished I was close to mine. I had seen so little of him once he and Mum were divorced, that we hardly had any kind of relationship at all.

"And how about you? What are your family like?" He probed.

Should I open up and tell him what he asked? It wouldn't hurt; it wasn't as if we were going to be great friends like Jack and I already were, so I guessed it would be fine.

"It's just Mum, me and my younger sister. Mum's been divorced a long time. We all get on well mostly. Mum's looks are similar to mine, but she is more beautiful. I have quite a bit of my dad in me. Mum is certainly more outgoing than I am, but she's rather eccentric." I grinned. "A bit reckless at times, but she's funny. She's my best friend, though we can argue like hell at times." He seemed to take in every syllable I uttered – as if I were the only person in the room. No one had ever paid me that much attention, and I liked it.

We chatted as we worked and I began to relax in his company. He had a natural, easy manner, but I was bewitched every time I gazed into those blue eyes. It sounds corny to say I was enchanted by him, but that was how I felt. It was a feeling I had never known before and hit me like an express train. I wondered what he thought of me, and then decided it might be best if I didn't know!

"Why is your mum on her own?" he asked, smudging some pencilled lines with his forefinger.

"Mum and Dad went their separate ways years ago, after deciding they were incompatible. Now, she just never seems to be able to meet the right one to remarry. She works in a school, but all the teachers are happily married, so she never gets a look in."

"That's a shame." He glanced between his reflection and the canvas, then back to me, then back to the canvas.

I was in disbelief that I'd just explained my dreary life to this rather posh and dishy guy who may or may not despise me. The whole time we were talking, Ashley Mason was concentrating on his sketching, but I noticed every so often that he was staring at me very directly. A tantalizing smile played round his lips.

Raising my eyebrows in surprise at his manner, I continued to study him covertly. I really hoped he wasn't noticing how interested in him I was. Most guys would never be interested in discussing anything so personal. Why had he come across to me so badly the other day? He seemed the complete opposite of the person I first saw in the student car park and I was more than pleasantly surprised. I knew I would be eager to get to school every day from now on, because I would see one Ashley Mason. But, of course, I had no chance with him, and that was very, very stupid of me to think otherwise.

❧ Five ❧

I realised I had been daydreaming a lot. All I could think about for the next few days was the memory of that art lesson … sitting next to Ashley … watching the movements of his perfect lips as we chatted … melting under the gaze of those gorgeous blue eyes and my own flickering back and forth to meet his gaze. I had managed a pretty thorough examination of him, and I liked what I saw. It was evident that he was curious about me, but was he interested in me? I had come to the conclusion that it was no good trying to work him out, or any male of the species. We girls just had to face the fact that guys were from a completely different planet – the Venus and Mars thing!

I was glad I was not the newcomer like Ashley, but I certainly wasn't as interesting as he was. I tried to disguise my interest in him by biting my lip, keeping a huge grin at bay. It was difficult for me to appear calm and detached. I was also curious about him and still wondered why he had given me that distasteful look in the student car park. That still bugged me … why had I repulsed him so? Of course, I knew deep down that it was my physical infirmity but I hadn't the guts to confront him about it. I didn't know him well enough yet. It could wait.

For a few days, Ashley was absent from art class. I couldn't ask anyone if they knew where he was without giving away the fact that I was interested in him. He was around somewhere, because I had seen his car in the car park. That was strange as well – he had begun parking on the other side, even though there was plenty of room where he usually parked, near to me.

Then, one lunchtime, I saw him in the dining hall with Nathan Cooper and Aimee. I tried to catch his eye but he was deeply involved in their discussion and didn't even look up. I watched as they got up from their table and left together, still chatting earnestly. Was it that he hadn't seen me, I wondered? Didn't want to see me, was more like it. He obviously regretted getting into conversation with me for some reason, and was avoiding me. Damn him; I was confused by his behaviour and wasn't sure how to react. I sighed deeply, my heart heavy with disappointment.

"What's up, Anna?" Jack asked. "You look right peed off with yourself today. Come out with me tonight, I'll soon cheer you up!"

He didn't deserve the murderous look I gave him.

"You okay? You've hardly said a word," Amelia added.

"I'm fine," I said, pushing my chair back and picking up my bag. "Is it a crime to be quiet now?"

"Where are you going?" Jack flashed a concerned glance at Amelia and began to get up at the same time.

"I need a book from my car," I lied.

"Shall I come with you?"

"Jack, will you just leave it!" I shouted and left the hall with as much dignity as I could muster, praying that my awkward feet wouldn't fall over each other, at least until I was well out of sight.

I reached my car safely and turned around. There were quite a few students coming and going and one or two groups having discussions but, thankfully, Amelia and Jack were nowhere to be seen. I knew I had behaved badly; they were my friends after all and had only wanted to help. I just wished they would give me a bit of space sometimes, that was all.

Where was Jess, I wondered? She usually joined us for lunch, complaining about the morning's "draggy" lessons and eyeing up possible dates for the weekend. I sat in my car, trying to make some sense of the emotional turmoil I was feeling. It was weird; I'd never felt like this before and wasn't sure how to deal with it. It was almost time for my lesson. I took a couple of deep breaths and told myself to get a grip and quit being so bloody stupid.

Leaving the car, I hoisted my bag onto my shoulder and picked my way warily across the potholed car park to my class. The breeze was getting up and as I raised my head to toss the hair out of my eyes, I saw Jess. She was leaning against the wall, deep in conversation...with Ashley Mason! God, no, she surely wasn't hoping to get a date with him, was she? Hadn't she heard what Jack had said "he definitely doesn't date"? I groaned inwardly, put my head down again and desperately tried not to think about it.

The afternoon lessons seemed never-ending and yet when the bell rang at home time I was reluctant to move. In a strange way, I had felt protected in my own small world while the teacher's voice droned on about global social and economic issues. I had just been another face in the class, not having to explain my thoughts or actions to anyone. In a few minutes I would have to face Amelia and Jack...and Jess, and try to behave normally. Well, I couldn't do that; it was impossible. I would shut them up by pretending a headache and needing an early night.

Amelia waited for my by the door. "What's the matter?" she asked, looking into my eyes.

"Just a headache. Don't fuss, I'll be fine when I've had a rest."

"From where I'm standing, it looks like more than just a headache."

"It's...you know, with the other pains as well, it's a bit much today."

Jack came rushing up to me. "Shall I come round later? My mum's on the late night shift, I'll bring my new CD—"

"Anna's got a headache, Jack," Amelia said quickly, sensing my discomfort.

"Oh, I'll leave the CDs until next time, then?"

"Not tonight, Jack, okay?" I said, attempting a weak smile.

There was no sign of Jessica. "Where's Jess?" I asked nonchalantly.

"In the library. Said there was something she needed to write."

"Oh, right." Like hell; when did Jess ever stay at school longer than she needed to? There was no doubt in my mind that she had arranged to meet Ashley and she thought the library story would be a plausible excuse. Well, I wasn't fooled by it and I realised that I might as well forget all about Ashley Mason; he wasn't going to be interested in me.

Later on, as I passed the drama studio on the way out, I did a double take. The doors were wide open and I could see Ashley in there with Miss Anderson and Mr Ridgeway and two or three more students. I didn't want to stop and stare, in case Ashley caught me, but they appeared to be lifting scenery boards into place. And Jess was upstairs in the library, waiting to meet him when he had finished whatever it was he was doing!

I knew I was letting myself down by allowing myself to get upset, but the tears came without warning and there were too many to hold back. What a fool I had been to daydream about a guy I never stood any chance with; he had only been so nice because he felt sorry for me. Then I recalled that look of revulsion that he had given me the first time I saw him. *That* was what he was really like.

I dragged a tissue across my cheeks in turn and then took a couple of deep breaths, trying to regain control. I threw my bag in the car, climbed in after it and fastened my seat belt for the drive home. Guess what? I really did have a splitting headache!

The next few days weren't so bad and everything seemed more or less normal, on the surface at least. I discovered that Ashley and a couple of other art students had been asked if they would like to help design and paint the scenery for the upcoming school production of *Mamma Mia,* which explained his absence from normal art classes. I was watching Jessica like a hawk, but she gave nothing away and I decided that she couldn't be secretly dating Ashley anyway; there was no way she would be able to keep quiet about it if that were the case. She did seem to be spending a lot of time writing notes in her book during lessons. That was a bit out of character, I thought, but I had now dismissed the idea that she and Ashley were together.

Ashley was back and had set up his easel with his self-portrait and had already begun sketching when I walked into art class a couple of days later. Glancing over, I noticed his posture stiffen. What was wrong? I thought it best to set my work up a distance away and let him get on with it. Mr Ridgeway gave his normal brief instructions as he moved around the class, checking out our work.

The trouble was, I could not stop myself from glancing in Ashley's direction, and every time our eyes met, his back stiffened. This continued for a while, as we both worked. I wondered if this was "normal" behaviour for a teenage boy. I was expecting him to settle down and relax, but he never did.

Why was everyone acting strangely today? Amelia hardly spoke to me in registration and wouldn't meet my gaze. She didn't even talk to me, apart from "Hi", and "Hope you have a good day". I knew this wasn't normal behaviour for her; especially not when it was aimed at me.

I was bewildered. Had I done something to upset everyone? I wasn't aware that I had. The art class seemed to drag. Even Jack hadn't spoken to me and kept giving me strange glances. For

Jack to treat me like that, there really must have been something seriously wrong. I was intrigued now as I glanced once more at Ashley and then immediately regretted it. He was glaring at me again. Those beautiful cobalt eyes had turned cold and full of revulsion. It was a replay of that encounter in the car park.

Surely it couldn't have been anything to do with me? I really didn't remember saying anything that would offend him the other day. Had I dreamt that he had been pleasant to me during that art lesson? Did that revealing conversation actually take place? Had he said more than he meant to? I was beginning to wonder. Ashley didn't even know me that well. The atmosphere was intolerable. I had to confront him and demand to know what his problem was.

Quietly as a shadow, I crept into his work space and stood a foot behind him. His back was turned towards me, so I couldn't read his expression.

In a low, almost inaudible voice, I asked him what his issue was. "You have been glaring at me all through the lesson. What have I done to you? My friends have been 'off' with me today as well. What's going on?" I hoped I wouldn't give away just how upset I was.

He turned round to face me slowly. He was obviously trying not to be noticed by the others, but already I could feel Jack's eyes burning into the back of my head.

"I'm sorry, Orianna, I can't speak about this right now. I do need to talk to you, though." His eyes bored into mine, as if he were trying to work something out. "I promise…I will. It's not your fault. It's me…sorry."

What the hell did that mean?

Then he turned away abruptly and I felt ignored as he continued with his work. Anger rose within me; I could feel it getting stronger. It was like fire and I could have burned him alive.

As soon as the bell rang, he started packing his stuff away. By the time I had gathered everything and stuffed it into my bag, Ashley had already gone. Unanswered questions were tumbling around in my head. Maybe it would be more prudent of me to forget about being his friend, and not even try. In the circumstances, it didn't seem like that was what he wanted any more. What had he meant...not my fault? What wasn't? What on earth did he need to talk about? I'd hardly seen him for about ten days. I decided he must suffer from mood swings; he was so different today, exactly like he was the first time I saw him in the student car park.

My frustration turned to anger and as Jack made for the door, I caught hold of his arm. He never ignored me, at least not like this. What had I done to *him*?

"Are you going to tell me what's going on?"

"Wha—? Oh, hi. Er..."

I could tell he was going to give me a load of bullshit. "Save it, Jack," I snapped. "Either give it to me straight or not at all. Right?" As my anger increased, my voice got louder.

He took me at my word. "Okay. Stay away from Ashley Mason. He's no good for you, Orianna. He will hurt you. I saw you talking to him in art. I know you won't believe me, but I promise he's not for you. Please, I'm telling you as a friend, stay away from him. That's all I'm going to say."

His tone was almost apologetic. He raised his palms at my face in order to stop the conversation dead in its tracks. This was not like Jack at all; he was normally so friendly, flirty even, like some kind of loyal lapdog who forever followed me around. Today he was a decidedly different person. What he'd just said didn't make any sense to me at all.

"What are you talking about?" I called after his retreating back. Oh, what was the use? I would get it out of Amelia tonight; she would tell me the truth. I hated secrets, especially when friends or family were involved. At the moment I felt as if my friends were involved in some conspiracy against me.

On my way to textiles, I met Amelia in the corridor. She tried to avoid my eyes, but I stopped in front of her, so that she couldn't avoid me. Other people hurried past on their way to class, but I didn't care if I was late. This needed to be resolved. I tried to stay calm as I stood directly in front of her.

"Amelia! Tell me what on earth is going on? Why are you and Jack acting so strange around me? Why is Jack warning me to stay away from Ashley Mason?" I tried to conceal the tremor in my voice as I looked at her intently.

She looked down, saying nothing.

I was so furious I could have hit her, which wasn't like me at all. "Well? I'm waiting for an answer."

She winced, making only brief eye contact with me.

"Sorry, Orianna, you'll have to speak to Ashley. I want nothing to do with this because I don't want you to get hurt. Please don't ask me about it. I'm always here for you as a friend, but *please* don't ask my advice about that Mason boy."

I could see that she didn't even want to look me straight in the eye, which worried me even more. I couldn't let this go.

"What do you mean?" My eyebrows knitted together in perplexed confusion.

"He and the 'it' crowd he hangs around with are bad news, you know that! Please take notice of me, I promised I will speak to you, I need to speak with you, just not now." she urged.

Before I could say any more, she slouched her shoulders, turned her back on me and disappeared into the horde of students as quickly as possible.

Now I was really irritated; pissed off, even. Amelia had never been like that with me all the time I had known her. I didn't know what to think.

The rest of the morning dragged on for what seemed an eternity, but I got through it. Should I seek Ashley out again and force him to tell me what was on his mind? Or wait until he was ready? Or perhaps it would be better to ignore him altogether? Yes, I could do that now and I damned well would!

After class finally finished, and everyone had gone to lunch, I noticed Ashley perching on the bonnet of his Audi. Red mist swirled around my head, but I was determined to disregard him and just calmly walk past him to collect some books from my car.

As I drew level with him, he stopped me abruptly by grabbing my hand and pulling me into his personal space.

I swore under my breath, with indignation. How dare he?

"What do you want?" I demanded, freeing myself from his grip. I really didn't want to talk to him after the way he had behaved this morning.

"I need to talk with you – to explain."

He frowned as he spoke, looking rather apologetic and hurt all at the same time. His cobalt eyes flickered, searching mine urgently as if trying to explain without words. I was lost. At the moment when our gazes locked he could have asked of me whatever he wanted and I would have surrendered. The intensity in his eyes was too much for me to ignore.

"Can we take a drive somewhere? I need to talk to you in private. That art lesson this morning nearly killed me, being so close to you and not being able to talk." His expression looked somewhat pained.

"But … " I began.

He stopped me short. "Please, Orianna. Hear me out?"

His tone confused me, as well as his apparent urgency in wanting to talk. And I was curious. I hated this feeling of not being in control of the situation, so I agreed to take a drive. No one would miss us, and we would have the lunch break to discuss whatever was on his mind.

As we pulled out of the school parking area, I noticed Nathan Cooper standing a few yards away from where we'd been. He looked really angry for some reason. At his side was Aimee, his recently acquired blonde bimbo girlfriend.

Neither of us knew what to say and the silence was deafening. The avenue of mature trees, mirror-imaged on either side of the road, raced past as I stared out of the window. The road ducked and dived like a roller coaster as we headed off and away from school, into the open countryside.

From the CD player floated some Muse track I recognised from one of the *Twilight* movies. I tried to relax, not wanting him to see the anxiety I knew showed in my face. My face was an open book. For that reason I was a hopeless liar. I wondered whether Ashley was going to lie to me about what was going on, or would he tell me the whole truth? I continued to wonder, as we pulled into the gravel track that led to Bradbury Rings.

I was relieved when he brought the car to a halt on the grass. I had been holding on tightly to the grab handle, as he did seem to drive faster than the speed limit allowed on the winding country roads.

The awkward silence continued as Ashley parked facing the point-to-point racecourse. It was a dull, cloudy day, somehow reflecting the moody atmosphere inside the car. Ashley kept fiddling with the CD player as he turned the volume down so that we could talk above it. He unclipped his seatbelt and turned in his seat to face me. I could feel his tension and tried to keep myself as relaxed as possible. I unfastened my seat belt and waited.

"This is really hard," Ashley said at last. "I don't know how to bring up the subject without offending you." He seemed very subdued. I was completely mystified and wished he would just get on with it and tell me whatever it was that was so hard to tell me.

He then took from his coat pocket a folded sheet of A4 paper. It was crumpled and creased from constant unfolding and refolding. He held it out to me.

"Please read this, it might explain a few things."

✎ Six ✎

I took the paper from Ashley and, under his intense scrutiny, I opened it. It was written on both sides in a familiar squirmy handwriting.

To Ashley:

If Orianna's disability seems an issue for you, you might be unsure about how to pursue her. As a friend of hers, this is how I see things.

Realise that she is just like every other girl! She has the same romantic dreams every other girl in the world has. She wants you to kiss her in the pouring rain, tickle her, hold her; she wants to fall in love, too. Just because she is physically disabled, that does not affect her hopes and dreams.

Don't treat her like she is stupid. She might be lacking in physical ability, but that does nothing to affect her mind, she's very intelligent AND artistic. And don't underestimate this girl either! You might be surprised… If you don't know what is wrong, or what her condition is, ask her. Make sure you're alone with her and just politely bring it up. I know she's answered all the questions millions of times and has the routine off pat. Don't worry that she'll get too emotional, because she probably won't. And even if you already know what's wrong, ask her anyway and get the whole story.

Make sure to plan activities that she can do. For example, don't go rock climbing, but go to a movie or concert.

Oh, and a word of advice, don't be overprotective. She doesn't need you to watch every step she takes, and she doesn't need your help with everything. Her mum is probably protective enough and Orianna knows how to handle herself. Instead of asking her about her "limitations", watch her (not in a creepy way either). If you know she has trouble getting in your car, give her your hand and help her, and so on, right? BE A GENTLEMAN! Just watch her and then you'll know when she needs a hand, then just give it to her without any fuss. The "thank you" will be the most heartfelt words you will ever hear.

If your friends want to know why she is the way she is, tell them when she isn't around so she doesn't get bombarded with questions. Yes, she's used to them, but the fact that she is physically disabled isn't important and shouldn't be the focus of the conversation.

Hardly believing what I was reading, I turned the page over.

Tips:

1.   Even Orianna wants romance! Hold her hand, snuggle together and kiss her passionately. Just do all the things you would do with any other girlfriend. That's if she likes you in THAT way.

2.   Don't try to make things "easier" for her; she likes a challenge, too. Realise that half the time she doesn't even think about what she can and can't do, so try to understand her and don't worry about it!

3.   Don't be afraid that you will "hurt" her, if you do, she'll tell you or you'll know by the look on her face!

4.   Just because she is disabled doesn't give you a reason to be an idiot at times, to ditch her for someone else, or to be "too nice". Don't feel sorry for her at any time because I know what she has been through and that has probably made her stronger.

5.   Realise that she will be ridiculed by ignorant people who don't even know her. She'll get stared at, laughed at and treated unfairly. Know that as her boyfriend or even her friend you are subject to criticism, too. Just ignore it because she probably does too by now, but don't fight all her battles for her; don't get all worked up. Let it slide unless she really shows that she's bothered or something or someone hurts her.

I really hope this helps. Talk to her, she is normal and a great girl. I should know – I'm her friend.

Jessica x

The note read more like an essay. My temperature rose with anger and I knew exactly what was meant by the expression "boiling with rage". The words were so typical of Jessica – melodramatic and cutting. Embarrassing, even! What the hell was she up to? I could feel my face flushing with embarrassment as I read and re-read the words. How could Jessica do this to me? Why on earth had she written this to Ashley? It was so patronising and condescending. I was too annoyed to even speak and just turned to Ashley and stared at him in disbelief. My shocked expression must have hit him like a brick. My face turned an indignant shade of crimson.

"Orianna, I know this looks really bad. You see, I asked Jessica about you. I…well, I wanted to get to know you, but I felt so unsure about…you see, Nathan and his mates are so ignorant. They just wouldn't be able to cope with you. They have such little understanding, it sickens me. I just wanted to understand you, and your disability and what it must be like to be...disabled." He looked away, clearly uncomfortable even expressing the word.

So that's what the tête-à-tête had been about when I saw Jess and Ashley outside the school and immediately jumped to the wrong conclusion! Not that I felt any better for knowing that; I was bloody annoyed.

"Why did you have to involve my friends? You could have asked me directly. I wouldn't have minded, you know. I might have been flattered, if you'd had the decency to ask me!" I jabbed the now folded letter under his nose abruptly and stared at him.

"I realise that now. But I was too embarrassed and...well, I didn't want you to judge me. I wanted an honest answer from your friends before I approached you. Then Jessica gave me this note. Amelia told me bluntly to speak with you directly, and Jack...well, Jack was over-protective and told me to leave you alone."

"Jack fancies me, that's his normal reaction," I retorted.

Ashley gave me a wry smile. "Yes, it was pretty obvious he was trying to warn me off."

"Do you think you should be warned off me, then?"

"No, not at all." He looked at me with uncertainty. "You see, I really like you."

My heart fluttered in the brief silence as he continued. I tried to fix my gaze on the clouds racing by in the sky overhead. I wanted to concerntrate on what he was saying; if I looked at him, I knew I would crumble and end up agreeing with everything he said, far too easily.

"Your disability is not a problem for me at all. It's everyone else's attitude around me that is the problem. I wouldn't care what other people thought of me for wanting to be with you, it's not that at all. I just don't want anyone causing you grief because I am interested in you. I'd hate to think of you being bullied and ridiculed because of me. What I would really like is to get to know you, spend time with you and see what happens. I'm open to possibilities, the possibilities of *us*."

Now, when he spoke, his eyes were soft and gentle. He paused, waiting for my reply.

"Don't be worried on my account," I told him. "I can handle the likes of Nathan Cooper." My gaze flickered over the letter that he was still holding in his hand. "And as for that step-by-step guide, I know Jessica meant well, but it seems you have been asking everyone else, except the one person you should have been talking to, *me*!"

I could feel my face reddening again. I hadn't felt as angry as this for a long time. "Everyone seems to talk about me like I'm a bloody science experiment or something, and I *hate* it!" I continued with feeling. "All disabled people like me want, and I include myself in this, is to be accepted for who we are and not because of our disabilities."

"Yes, I realise that," Ashley answered warily, probably wondering where the conversation was heading next.

"That is all I want," I parroted, "for people to accept me for who and not what I am, but unfortunately the world we live in is shallow and so many people judge by outward appearances."

By now I was raising my voice again, and needed to take a breath and calm down. "Because of the way I am, I lack confidence," I continued. "I know that if I wasn't like this, I'd be really feisty, and very probably a complete bitch, right up myself, much like Nathan's new bit of stuff."

I sighed with relief that whatever else I might be, I was *not* a bitch.

"You talk about *us*," I continued, "but you know so little about me." I wasn't sure what his response would be, but I would listen – that was all I could do. He pawed his hand nervously through his dark hair.

"I'd just like us to get to know each other and see how things go between us, that's all I'm saying. Underneath it all I am quite shy, you know." He lowered his head, looking at me sheepishly through dark, curly lashes. "Guys hate the thought of rejection too, you know."

I laughed at that remark. "You seem to *know* an awful lot. I agree that Jessica meant well. She just has a strange way of going about things. No wonder she and Jack have been funny with me." I waved the letter in front of him again. "Do you *know* that Jess hasn't been able to speak to me or even look me in the face today? Now I understand why. It's because, whatever their faults, they are good mates and are just looking out for me, so you will just have to accept that."

Ashley was smiling. What the hell did he find so amusing? I toyed with the screwed-up note in my hand, trying to decide if I needed to tear it into small pieces or hand it back to him. I was about to launch another verbal attack, but his next remark completely took the wind out of my sails.

"You seem so generous and good-natured. I love that about you," he stated.

My anger subsided. *I love that about you.* He'd just said those words...to *me*! And they made me feel great, even though I hardly knew him. The wind whipped around the outside of the car, but I somehow felt comfortable and safe. Physically, I was cocooned in the luxury of twenty-first century engineering; mentally, I was close to heaven. I had to admit to myself that being in close proximity to Ashley was amazing, and up until this moment had been unthinkable.

I felt empowered, suddenly. His words melted into me; as if they were affirming themselves under my skin as he spoke. Now I was beginning to understand, and I wanted to cuddle him so that my face, my cheek, my hair, became a part of him and I could feel I belonged for the first time in my life. Something extraordinary was happening to me. My feelings of anger were becoming disentangled. The initial feelings of revulsion for his attitude started to wane. I seemed to be opening up my feelings to him and, for the very first time, I was beginning to feel accepted by a man.

We lapsed into silence again, but this time it was meaningful, not strained and awkward as it had been earlier. Something had changed; the tension dissipated and we were both relaxed, taking pleasure from the moment of being together, watching clouds race across the sky, a world away from school and notes and jealous friends.

"Maybe you should stay away from me," I mused, still gazing into the heavens. I wanted to gauge his emotional reaction. I snuggled against his shoulder as an arm curled around mine.

His answer was sharp. "Why ever would I need to do that?"

"I don't want you losing your friends because of me. People will judge you for being with me, you know, ridicule you, even." I screwed my face up as I made the remark, just to drive it home.

"If you don't mind me asking a personal question, what exactly is your disability?"

"I have cerebral palsy. If you want more technical info, ask your dad, or you can Google it!"

"That is very straight and to the point!" Ashley said with an embarrassed giggle.

He nudged me with his hand.

"Don't be so down on yourself. I've not had a friend with CP before. I know nothing about the condition."

I was glad he was finally questioning me to my face , even though he was a bit unsure. I got fed up with being serious all the time, but once I'd explained things, I knew I wouldn't have to explain again. I grinned back at him.

"You sound so serious – I just don't like explaining it to people all the time. I was born prematurely. I was so tiny and starved of oxygen, it affected me like this. I have been like it all my life," I explained, looking directly up at him so that I could measure his reaction.

"Sorry to come across as ignorant, but how does it affect you, physically, I mean?" I could feel his arm around me more tenderly now.

"I'm in pain most of the time. It's like I am constantly walking on a bed of nails. The pain sometimes makes me irritable. If I get like that my friends have to rein me in and I understand that. I know it must be a bore."

"But friends should make allowances for you and try to understand. I'm sure they wouldn't want to be like you?"

I shook my head. "Don't pity me, Ashley. I don't want pity." I tried not to be snappy or condescending; I just wanted to get my point across.

He reached for my hand, with his free arm. "No, no. I don't pity you at all. People pity what they don't understand. I admire your strength and courage. I think you are amazing and I wish more girls were like you. They depend on us guys too much, can't think for themselves and feel the need to be preoccupied with their outward appearance. What counts is how you should treat people and how they respond to you."

I said it again. "Acceptance is what I strive for – to be accepted for being me and not a disability!"

The only "person" in my life whom I felt had truly accepted me for who I was, so far in my life, was God, although I did have a tendency to call on him only when I needed divine intervention. This was a rare occurrence as, being stubbornly independent, I thought I could do everything myself.

"Everyone wants acceptance, to be liked for who they are. I do!"

I smiled back at him, feeling relaxed once more. "It's your friends I worry about!"

"Let me handle them. I will deal with them in my own time and in my own way. All I am asking is that you give me a chance to be your friend. Sometimes, you seem to come across as moody and distant. But I know now that you're not like that. I can see that it's because of the pain you are in and I also see that you like to keep people at a distance. Your attitude is just a mask to avoid getting hurt. You are not the bad girl in this situation at all, it's other people's attitude to disabilities and that's their problem, not yours."

Now he was coming close to sounding patronising, but I knew that was not his intention. It was like he was almost begging, as he said all this, as if by stressing the point, he would somehow convince me that he was right. Of course, in my heart, I knew he was right. I hadn't realised what an effect I'd had on him. But then he didn't realise the profound effect he had on me!

We both stared out of the window after that, not quite knowing what to say next. I sat back in my seat, unlocking my hand from his, and watched the grey clouds playing catch-up across the sky.

Ashley broke the silence. "Sorry," he said, hesitantly, "I suppose we ought to get back?"

I looked at my watch and realised we had spent all afternoon together. God! I was going to be in trouble; skipping lessons wasn't usually my style.

Pulling up alongside my car in the school car park, Ashley applied the handbrake and turned to face me.

"Thanks for coming. I think we understand each other a little better now, don't you?"

I released my seat belt. "Yes," I agreed, reaching for my bag. "I guess we do."

As I turned to negotiate my exit from his car as gracefully as possible, he caught my hand. "Orianna?"

I faced him. Those eyes could weaken the strongest resolve. "Yes?"

"We can be friends…you and I. Can't we? I say this is between us, and our respective friends will have to accept it."

I smiled at him. He looked so intense and I felt his hand tighten around mine.

"Yes," I said. "I would like that."

Relief flooded his face and a smile spread across it, reaching the eyes, which twinkled gloriously. "Great. See you at art class, then?"

I slid out of his car. "Look forward to it!"

I slammed the door shut and with a toot on the car horn and a quick wave, he was gone.

I faced the fact that Ashley did seem to be too good to be true. He made the right gestures and said the right things but I didn't want our friendship to go wrong. I had to distance myself and keep my emotions in check until I really knew who this guy was. I just found it hard to believe that someone like Ashley would actually be interested in me. But perhaps he wasn't? If that were the case, would I be disappointed? I couldn't tell. There were too many different emotions and I couldn't cope with them. It would certainly surprise a few people if they knew about our meeting. But I didn't care what anyone thought, I just knew that a few things needed to be sorted out and that was it.

I threw my bag in the car and headed off home, hoping no one had missed me.

❧ Seven ❧

I was normally first to get home from school, but Mum and Izzey were already in when I reached home. Izzey was sprawled across the sofa, cuddling Gio and watching TV.

"Was the traffic bad, love?" Mum asked, bringing her cup of tea into the lounge. If she didn't have a ciggy in her hand it was a cuppa instead.

"No more than usual on a Friday."

"You're later than usual, aren't you?"

"So I got held up." I had no intention of giving even a hint of why I was late home. I left the two of them in the lounge and took my bag upstairs. Sitting on the side of my bed, my thoughts went back to the afternoon, spent with Ashley. I really didn't know what to make of the situation. That note Jess had written to him was the limit; why did she have to go and write down all that stuff about me? And why keep it a secret from me? Most friends would tell you if a boy was asking about you…make an issue out of it, but she had chosen to tell Jack and Amelia instead of me. That annoyed me, and yet I knew they were all good mates and only wanted what was best for me.

Fumbling in my coat pocket, I pulled the now very crumpled paper out and opened the note, my eyes dancing over the words, still unable to take them all in. I tossed the page into the bin in indignation.

The first time I set eyes on Ashley, I knew he was special somehow, and then he had stared at me so rudely in the car park that I began to have second thoughts, though no one could dispute that he was extremely fanciable. He had blown hot and cold during our encounters in art class, and now he professed to want me as a friend. Was that all...a friend, or did he mean girlfriend? After skim reading Jess's note, it had appeared to refer to me as a potential girlfriend, but that didn't necessarily mean that was how Ashley saw me. I could hardly go up to him and say, "Oh, hi, Ashley. You know you were interested in having me as your friend? Did you mean your girlfriend by any chance?"

I thought he was interested in dating me, but I couldn't be sure, and I wasn't going to go and ruin everything by pushing it, so I would just have to wait and see what happened next. Meanwhile, I would play it cool. And I would treat my friends Amelia, Jack and Jess in the same way...yeah, cool as a cucumber.

Mum's voice from the bottom of the stairs broke into my thoughts. "Orianna! Amelia's on the phone, love." I wriggled off my bed and went to pick up the upstairs phone in Mum's room.

"Hi, Anna. You okay? Where did you get to this afternoon?"

Here we go. "Oh, er, I had stuff to see to," I said nonchalantly.

"We were worried, especially when Jack said he thought we'd upset you. We all tried ringing you, but your mobile was switched off."

I had completely forgotten about my mobile phone. I'd kept it on silent earlier, not wanting the embarrassment of answering any awkward questions in Ashley's presence.

"Anna?"

"What?"

"Are you mad with me? *Did* we upset you?"

"I did wonder what was going on, but no, you didn't."

"Um, have you seen Ashley at all?"

I really wasn't prepared to discuss any of this, especially with Mum and little sister's ears flapping not far away. "Why? Should I have?"

"I just wondered..."

"What are we doing tomorrow, anyway?" I asked quickly.

"Oh, well, Jack's got a new DVD and his mum and dad are going out for the evening, so we're invited to his place. Jess has got a date."

"Anyone we know?"

"It'll be a different guy again next week, anyway, so it doesn't really matter!"

We giggled and gossiped together and any awkwardness was forgotten by the time we rang off. It looked like another evening spent at Jack's then.

The following week took care of itself. The atmosphere between Jack, Amelia and I had calmed down. They knew something was 'going on' with Ashley and I, yet they were wise not to push me on it. Amelia knew I would confide in her if I wanted too, when the time was right. Jack, well he sulked a little and seemed to then be the same as always – his normal flirty self.

Ashley was helping me to pack up after art class when he said, "Are you rushing off straight away?"

"I needn't. Why?"

"Mr Ridgeway wants to see me about the scenery for the play. Could you wait for me in the car park?"

Had I heard right? He wanted me to wait for him... my heart did its usual acrobatics and then began its pounding. "Okay."

"Great. See you in a bit." He handed me my bag and gave me a delightful wink as he walked off. I tried not to blush as I watched his gorgeous arse go out the door.

I waited inside my car, not wanting to look too conspicuous. Ashley was only about 15 minutes and I spent the time deleting old voicemails and text messages from my mobile phone. If anyone saw me, they would assume I was busy phoning or texting and wouldn't think it so strange that I was sitting on my own in the car park.

I saw him walking towards me and opened the car window.

"Thanks for waiting," he said. "Can I get in for a minute?"

He looked serious and I wondered what was on his mind. "Sure."

He dumped his bag on the tarmac and slid into the seat next to me, leaving the car door open.

"How's the scenery coming along?" I wanted to appear relaxed and interested.

He nodded. "Oh, yes, it's going very well. Almost finished now." He motioned to my phone. "Sorry, were you…?"

"No, it's okay."

He cleared his throat. "Orianna, I wanted to ask you something. Erm…"

"What is it?"

He grinned. "Well…look, it's the weekend tomorrow. Would you let me take you out for the day? Bring your sketchbook and art materials and perhaps we could do some sketching? Please come, it will give us a chance to talk. I promise to be a gentleman. I *can* be nice, contrary to what you may have been led to believe. I'd just like the chance to spend some time with you, to talk."

His expression was anxious, yet hopeful. I supposed it wouldn't hurt. We were friends now, after all. At least it might help me to understand what Amelia and Jack had been going on about and I didn't want to fall out with either of them again, so perhaps this was a way of avoiding that. It was now obvious that things had been said between Ashley, Amelia and Jack, and I really needed to try and get my head round the situation once and for all.

"What are you thinking?" he asked anxiously.

I smiled, feeling confident enough to answer his question.

"Yep, okay, I will. I'll spend time with you tomorrow, on the understanding that you talk to me so I can understand *you* better," I retorted.

He put all my contact details into his iPhone, we made arrangements where and when to meet, and said goodbye. My heart was fluttering in my chest and I wondered whether I had done the right thing by agreeing to go. However, I decided to look upon it as a necessity. It was the perfect opportunity for me to get at the truth.

The next day, anticipation in my heart was immense as I prepared to meet up with Ashley. I had no idea where we would go, or what he would have to say for himself. In and out of the shower, wide awake now, I gave some thought to what I should wear. Something casual but pretty? Yes, that should fit the bill. In the end, after trying a few ensembles, I decided that the white cotton t-shirt felt fresh against my smooth skin. Trimmed with a delicate lace edging, it was a favourite of mine. A pale pink oversized cardigan from M&S, teamed with jeans and casual loafers completed my outfit.

Next, I opened the "Twitterrific" application on my mobile and wrote a post on my profile: "Out meeting someone for a chat today … I will let you know how it goes … laters x"

Twitter was the latest social networking site, with real celebrities, actually talking about real events in their lives. You could "follow" them or they could even become a "follower" of you. I had already added a bio of myself, with a picture included, so that people could see who I was. Jonathan Ross and his wife, Jane Goldman, were following me, amongst others, which was bizarre but rather fun. I had a few "ordinary" followers, too. Of course, I was following all the real celebrities on there, Russell Brand, Stephen Fry, Julie Moore (the celebrities' clairvoyant), Joyce Meyer the evangelist, to name but a few. Anyway, would there be any comments posted to me about "What am I doing?" I would have to wait and see, but I was giving no details away yet.

Gio was lying on my bed, watching me tidy up, after I'd thrown every item of clothing I owned across my room. She seemed to know she would be spending some time on her own. I felt guilty about it, but I couldn't exactly take her with me today.

Time was ticking on and I needed to be out of the house, ready for Ashley to collect me. I grabbed a bag, some drawing materials and sketch book, and headed downstairs, checking my make-up in the hall mirror. I looked as presentable as I could without overdoing it and categorised myself as casual but cute.

Mum had already left to go clothes shopping with her friend and Izzey was at her friend's house again. Neither of them knew what I was up to today, and nor did Jack and Amelia. In a way, that was good; I didn't want them to know in case they misconstrued it as a date. Mum jumped to conclusions, so that would be exactly what she'd think. Then there would be too many questions to answer and she would also have too many expectations of Ashley. Everything was best left unsaid, for the time being at least, until I knew what was happening.

Mum, as usual, had forgotten to switch the dishwasher on, so I did that and made sure Gio had fresh water. I was just about to empty the pedal bin when the door bell rang. I suddenly felt nervous and took my time answering the door, but when I saw Ashley standing before me, nothing else mattered. My heart did its usual somersault in his prescence and my achey knees felt weaker than normal, but at the same time I felt fantastic. Was this what an instant hit of heroin felt like? For sure, I was suddenly higher than the proverbial kite as I took in his gorgeous eyes and tousled hair and caught a waft of his exclusive aftershave – probably the one that was known as sex in a bottle. My thoughts were racing. He left me breathless; I only had to think of him to totally lose any sense of where I was or what I was doing.

It would be difficult, but I knew I had to try and retain a sense of detachment, because he must never realise that I did actually fancy him. He gave me that disarming smile and held out a huge spray of flowers. Not your ordinary bunch of cellophane wrapped, either – these had been carefully selected and professionally packaged to impress.

"Thank you, it's great to see you," I chirped. Not knowing what else to say, I mumbled something about finding a vase and showed him into the lounge.

Gio came hurtling down the stairs and jumped up to greet him.

"Hey, this must be your dog. She is so friendly." He tried to calm her by letting her damp nose sniff his hand.

"Yes, she is. She will calm down in a minute, don't worry, she just wants to say hi."

He seemed to be perfectly at ease with her, which was good to see. "It's fine, honestly, I love animals. Do you mind if I sit down?" Gio tried to jump on him before he even got comfortable.

By the time I had arranged the flowers and tidied up the kitchen worktop, Gio and Ashley had made friends and were getting on famously. She sat cheekily on his lap, vying for attention, planting sneaky little kisses on his arm and chin with her tongue. He looked so relaxed and didn't seem fazed by anything. Thank goodness he liked animals.

"Come on, Gio, get down, now!" I raised my voice and she complied.

"You have a really nice place here," he said, glancing round the room. Your mum has good taste. It's really comfortable and cosy."

"Thanks, I noticed you were sat quite comfortably!" I grinned at him.

"Shall we make a move?" he suggested. "I've planned a lot today and don't want you to miss a thing."

"Sounds great!" I answered, wondering what surprises the day held.

"Did you pack your art stuff?"

"Yes, of course I did. You asked me to, though I'm not sure why?"

"You'll see."

He smiled. I melted. He took my bag from me, as if it were the most natural thing to do.

"Let's go," I said, pocketing my house keys.

Once outside, Ashley confidently guided me to his car and held the passenger door open for me. His hand in the small of my back was neither intrusive nor patronising, but made me feel fussy inside.

With the CD player at low volume, we passed through the town and headed off down the winding country roads towards Cranborne. I was not paying that much attention to the road ahead. I kept sneaking glances at Ashley beside me, confidently in command of the car. He was very relaxed today, perhaps because he felt more in control after our talk. And we were alone, so there was no one to judge us, or him in particular. I kept wondering whether or not he was bothered by my disability. I remembered his dark looks from earlier on, which were still baffling me. I knew his friends would have issues, especially if they knew I was in contact with him out of school. Nathan Cooper, in particular, would have a problem. His attitude to life was appalling; sex, drugs and rock 'n' roll, flavoured with selfish arrogance summed him up.

The hedgerows raced by and little thatched cottages shaped boldly into view, then blurred as we passed them. Overhanging clouds threatened rain. I hoped it would brighten up. My body shivered at the thought of sitting in the open, trying to sketch in the pouring rain. I tried to think of something to discuss with Ashley, so that we could get to know each other better. Then I decided to break the pleasant silence.

"Why are you friends with Nathan Cooper?" I had to know what it was about Nathan that attracted his friendship.

"I don't really know now, to be honest. He was great at first, fun to be around, and, of course, I was the new boy and he knew everyone. His background is similar in terms of his family's lifestyle, but that's where the similarities end."

"That's why I asked. You seem so different."

He focused on the road ahead as he continued.

"His values are entirely different from mine – you would probably call him a male chauvinist. The friendship has run its course really. It's not working for me any more and I'd prefer to have more down to earth friends, like you." He quickly glanced at me, giving me that delicious quirky smile.

When I smiled back, his hand left the steering wheel and held mine and for a while we drove along with our fingers entwined, hands resting just above his left knee. Although the move was unexpected, I felt comfortable with it and enjoyed the physical contact as I gradually responded and became more relaxed.

Shortly afterwards he returned to safe driving mode and resumed his hold on the wheel. This left my hand precariously on his thigh. I felt myself blushing as Ashley turned to me and smiled. If I was translating the body language correctly, he wanted more from me than friendship. So not all he said was strictly accurate, but a slight understatement of what he actually wanted. How could I read the signs right when I had never even had a boyfriend, and my mum's relationships never lasted long enough for me to be able to get to know the men involved, let alone have any understanding of them?

Now I had butterflies in my stomach and my heart was pounding because I knew that this was going to be an auspicious day – the start of what I was hoping would be something pretty amazing.

Ashley turned the car off the road onto a gravel track and parked.

"Where's this?" I asked.

"Knowlton Church. It's a local spot where I come to contemplate, relax and sketch."

"I've never been here before."

Ashley then went into great historical detail about the site.

"It's the ruins of a fourteenth-century church in the centre of a pagan earth circle." He motioned at the circle.

"If my research is correct it dates from when 'Christianisation' of the site took place by the earliest papal ministries. Apparently, it was a thriving community but the village suffered when it was virtually wiped out by the bubonic plaque. All that remains of the village today are vague traces of the foundations in a field a few hundred yards from the church."

He paused for a moment and pointed. "Yes, somewhere over there, I think. And despite the dreadful epidemic, the church itself continued in use until the early part of the eighteenth century. In or around 1747 the church was given a new roof, which promptly fell in! The church was abandoned and left to fall into ruin." His lecture ended.

"Wow, you are an encyclopaedia! Isn't it a shame it's all been left as a ruin? It must have been a lovely village at some point."

"Yes, I'm sure it was, and I believe they used to hold an annual fair, attracting villagers from miles away. It would have been quite an event."

Ashley certainly knew his local history. It was interesting to know what appealed to him and what knowledge he had. He seemed like an old head on a young body... a bit like me.

"You're obviously interested in history, then?" I asked.

"I enjoy history as much as drawing. I'm studying history at A-level as well as art."

"Hmm, I see. I like history too, but it clashed with fashion design so I couldn't study it at A-level. Fashion history is about the closest I get! My mum loves history, too. She got her degree with the Open University. But she doesn't look at local history, more British and world history."

"It would be nice to get to know your mum. She could help me with some of my essays," Ashley hinted with a grin.

It was reasonably warm and sunny for the time of year. Warm enough to sit with a coat on and sketch, anyway. After parking close by, we walked over to the ruins of the church. There was hardly anything of it left standing, except the bell tower and part of the walls. The rest, without a roof, was open to the elements.

"Would you like to stay here for a while and sketch?" Ashley asked. "I brought some folding chairs for us to sit on. It's a bit too damp to sit on the grass, and anyway, I thought you'd find it more comfortable."

"That was very thoughtful of you."

He had taken Jessica's advice very seriously. He had thought of everything…I didn't need to ask for anything. I wished I knew how to loosen him up. Hopefully he wouldn't be so serious as I got to know him better. Perhaps he was just nervous? It was a possibility.

We walked around the ruins, looking for good vantage points for our sketching.

"So this is where you come to think?" I asked him. "Do you have much to have to get away from?"

"Just the bustle of home, really. Dad's always working and Mum's either lunching with ladies, fund-raising or working. My sister and brothers are tied up with university or school. There's always somebody's friends popping in." He smiled. "Our house is a free for all. Mum and Dad say we should always make people welcome."

"Oh, sounds interesting having so many friends coming and going. My house is always quiet unless my sister brings her friends round. Incidentally, how did you know the church ruins were here in the first place?"

The smile still played around his lips. "I only live around the corner, near Witchampton, not ten minutes from here. I come here to get away, be alone if I need to."

"Oh. I didn't realise you lived out this way. I assumed you lived in Wimborne." I watched him through my lashes, hardly believing that I was alone with him – completely alone.

"How do you fancy coming round to my place afterwards, for lunch? No one's there today, they've all gone off to some charity function. I can make you some lunch and we could just relax and hang out together. What do you think?" He suddenly sounded more serious.

I was sketching Ashley as he sat drawing the ruins. I studied his face as I sketched, using a soft graphite pencil. The breeze curled around and under my jacket, making me pull it closer around me.

"Yes, that would be nice," I answered. "So long as I'm not in anyone's way. I mean, I won't be disturbing anyone?"

A puzzled frown creased Ashley's forehead. "Why would you be in the way? Why on earth would you disturb anyone? There's no one home, I promise."

"I just don't want to feel uncomfortable or awkward."

"You won't be in the way, or disturb anyone. You and I are friends now, so no one will have the right to make you feel like that, nor should they!"

I was not used to feeling included, especially not by the "it" crowd, so this was all new to me. I was a little nervous at the thought of entering his world face on. But I liked the idea of being with him so much that I was sort of looking forward to it, too.

The weather improved as we chatted. It was not so windy now and the sun was beginning to win its battle with the clouds. It made me feel alive, being out in the open air. I found this place refreshing and stimulating. I could hear the birds calling to each other in nearby trees, and there were rabbits in an adjacent field, pausing to listen and observe and then scurrying in all directions, flicking their trademark little white tails.

Ashley finished his sketch of the church. His drawing skills were truly exceptional; his work had a photographic quality.

"Now I've finished this, I'm going to do a sketch of you. Do you mind?"

I could read the question in his caring blue eyes: *Will it embarrass you?* The corners of his mouth curled up into a shy grin. I melted, of course.

"Why not? Let's see how good your portrait work is! I haven't got a good side though. You will have to do your best," I laughed.

Ashley laughed with me. "You haven't got a bad side either, you are beautiful."

"Don't say that!" I rebuked him.

"Why ever not? You are the most beautiful girl I have ever met. It's a shame you don't see what I see!"

Suddenly, he rose from his seat and moved it right next to mine. Now I could smell his aftershave, which was sweet and almost hypnotic. He put his hand in mine and began caressing it with the other hand as he turned to face me. He looked intently into my eyes.

"You are the most beautiful girl I know. I love your kind-hearted nature and you are generous, forgiving and patient. You always have time for everyone. You never seem to judge. Most of all, you don't judge me." Little did he know how angry I'd been with him days before. I was so glad he didn't have the ability to read my mind, otherwise I knew he wouldn't be talking to me like this. I felt guilty for judging him so badly.

He held my face gently in both hands. The effect on me was profound. In that moment, I felt as if a surge of electricity had coursed through my body. Ashley continued to gaze intently into my eyes, unaware of what I was feeling. Completely overwhelmed by his proximity to me, I could say nothing. His smell, his touch, his sensitivity...had my face been a bar of Galaxy, it would surely have melted.

"I don't care about your disability, how many times do I have to repeat myself, until you believe me?" he said flatly. My family brought us up to believe everyone was the same underneath, regardless of outward appearances. I have to be honest – I worried about it at first, because of what my friends thought, but for no other reason. You are such a great girl and our friendship means a lot to me. I want to get to know you more. Be there for you. Understand what is going on in your head."

His hands were resting on my shoulders now, but the deep blue gaze was steady as he put the finishing touches to my character reference.

"I admire your strength and your enthusiasm for life, your artistic talent and...your acceptance of me, despite the friends I hang out with."

I just smiled because I didn't know what to say. I was amazed at what I was hearing and he was so open and honest, which warmed my heart.

"So now would you like to go back to my house? It isn't far. We could have some lunch, listen to music. Chill out and watch a DVD perhaps? Whatever you'd like."

"Will your parents be there?" I wondered about the implications if his family were to be at home. Explanations, introductions and a certain amount of embarrassment. I winced, thinking about it. I hated having to explain to people about my disability. I also did not want to be judged. I was never confident when meeting new people. I was actually quite shy until I got to know them well enough to feel relaxed and free to be myself. I was apprehensive at the thought of going to Ashley's home and meeting his parents, but as he was now a good friend it seemed the next, most natural step.

"No," he said, playfully stroking my cheek. "Like I said, they're all out today."

We packed up our belongings. Ashley folded up the chairs and stowed them in the boot. Ten minutes later, we arrived at his home.

❧ Eight ❧

As we pulled up on the gravel drive, I saw instantly that it was no ordinary house. To me it was like a small mansion; something out of a Georgian novel, like Elizabeth Bennett's family home in *Pride and Prejudice*. It was awe-inspiring. I tried not to appear fazed by it, but I don't think Ashley was fooled by my efforts to be cool and casual. The house was timeless. An ivory coloured vision, three storeys tall, with working sash windows, it looked like it had undergone a lot of restoration.

"Wow!" was all I could say.

Ashley smiled. "You like it?"

"It's *amazing*. I didn't think houses like this existed in small country villages."

"I think it once belonged to landed gentry around here – probably a small country cottage to them. I don't know much of the history. Dad could tell you."

I was still rooted to the spot, completely blown away by Ashley's family home.

"Ready to go in?" he asked gently. "There's no one there. I promise, it's just us."

Guiding me by the elbow, we walked from the car to the front porch, which was partially obscured by a billowing old wisteria. I was sure that Ashley could detect my tension. I wasn't good with new situations, always needing time to adapt.

He opened the door and showed me in. The inside of the house was even more surprising. It was as stunning as the exterior. Ashley's mum was obviously a Laura Ashley fan, if the furnishings were anything to go by. The walls were painted in tasteful, muted colours and everything was colour coordinated, right down to the flowers in an ivory vase on the hall table. The house was straight out of *Ideal Home* or *Country Living*. Every room Ashley showed me into was immaculate and smelled of a fresh summer meadow.

We reached the kitchen. Ashley put the kettle on and placed two mugs on the glossy granite worktop.

"Tea?"

I nodded. "Thanks, that would be lovely. I never say no to a cup of tea"

After he made the tea, we wandered through to an adjacent sitting room. Not a main room of the house, but a small hideaway leading off from what might be termed a salon, or perhaps a drawing room. It was a cosy, quiet little area, more casually presented than the rest of the house.

We sat next to each other; rather awkwardly at first, although the sofa was soft and inviting. The house was very quiet; as we sipped our tea in silence, we could hear the ticking of a nearby clock. I didn't mind the peacefulness of the place, it was something different.

"Sorry it's all a bit formal," Ashley said. "Mum does a lot of entertaining, fund-raising and the like, so she likes everything just so. I like it when she doesn't have guests, when it's more lived in, like a home."

"It must be wonderful to live in the countryside like this, so close to nature with no traffic or street noise?"

"Yes, it's great. You notice the changing seasons a lot more as well. The sounds are different in the countryside; you hear the odd car driving past and at night there are owls and foxes calling."

"Where's your toilet?" I asked, rather embarrassed.

"I'll show you."

When I returned from the little girls' room he had produced a plateful of sandwiches, another one of cakes, and more tea.

"I hope you'll eat something?" he said. "I don't want you to feel hungry."

"You're very thoughtful."

"No, I just like to treat others how I would want them to treat me."

I bit my lip, thinking back to the way he treated me that day in the car park. Should I tackle him about it?

"What's wrong? Have I done something to upset you?"

"Well, yes." I said, rather sheepishly.

"What is it?

"A while ago, when we first saw each other, in the school car park, you looked at me as if I was dirt on your shoe, or even worse. At the time I didn't know you, and could see no reason why you should seem so offended by me. I was puzzled by it, and still am, to be honest."

"I didn't realise you were so observant." He looked down. "I'm sorry."

Puzzled, I let him continue.

"I looked at you because I couldn't understand how someone with your stunning looks could end up having such a physical disability." He pointed towards the ceiling. "Whoever makes the rules up there must be downright cruel... sadistic, even. Seeing someone with your disabilities made me realise just how self-centred my attitude was becoming. Measuring my own life against what others have or don't have sometimes brings me back to reality with a jolt! I swear I meant no offence by looking at you. And it wasn't about pity either, but rather admiration."

I couldn't believe what this guy was saying to me. People normally looked at me with disgust or revulsion, so for someone like Ashley to say I was stunning was the last thing I had expected. I sat there wide-eyed with my mouth open.

"Are you okay?"

I was, in a stunned sort of a way. "That's the nicest thing anyone has ever said to me," I replied, choking back my emotion.

I got up and crossed to the large window that overlooked the gardens and stared out, mulling over Ashley's comments. Maybe I was at fault, too. I condemned people who were quick to judge and yet I always judged peoples' expressions and preconceptions of me, without a second thought that they might actually be thinking the exact opposite.

"Oh no," Ashley groaned. "I've offended you again. I'm rubbish at this truth stuff. I'm so sorry."

He came to my side at the window and gently rested his arm across my shoulders.

"No," I assured him, "you haven't offended me. I do prefer people to talk to me and ask me questions about my disability, rather than remaining ignorant. Ignorance kills people, intellectually."

He nodded. "Quite."

"So how did you come to get that note from Jessica, then?" Now I was starting to probe.

"Well, I wasn't sure how my interest in you would be construed. I also wanted to be aware of how to treat you, so as not to make you feel uncomfortable or uneasy. You see, ignorance led me to ask those questions. I was way too shy and embarrassed to ask you directly, for fear of rejection or anger, I suppose. Asking Jessica seemed the right thing to do at the time."

"Why would you suppose I'd be angry with you? I am one of the most placid people you could meet. Nothing fazes me. For the umpteenth time, I just crave acceptance. For people to accept me the way I am."

He smiled. "I guess that's what we all strive for."

I observed him for a moment as he stood close to me, watching that slight flutter of his eyelashes as he smiled. God, he was gorgeous. It was hard to believe that someone with his looks, lifestyle and talent would have trouble being accepted. I mused to myself that someone so perfect couldn't be real – that he might disappear in a sudden puff of smoke, and this conversation would evaporate.

"You think *you* are so ordinary, Ashley. Well, believe me when I say you are far from that! Why do you worry so much about other people's opinions?"

"Don't we all do that?"

"Yeah, I guess we do," I agreed. "Do you care what your friends think of you?"

He still had his arm around my shoulders but I sensed rather than felt him flinch a little. However, the electricity between us was still evident and its effect on me was intense and sensual ... hypnotic, almost.

"Well, let's say I have my own opinions, but I don't like to rock the boat."

"Whatever do you mean?"

"Well, take Nathan, for example. If he knew you and I were friends, he'd be mad. He'd never understand because he is ignorant and more self-centred than most. What Nathan wants he gets, regardless. He would never understand a relationship of mutual respect like ours."

So was he declaring himself? Was it friendship he wanted or a relationship? I had to know.

"What do you want from me? I mean, what are you expecting to happen between us?" I asked, tentatively, almost scared of his reply.

He gazed down at me, playfully fingering through my hair. Again I felt that frisson of intense pleasure at his touch.

"Orianna, I don't ever want to hurt you. All I want is to be able to love you. I couldn't live with myself if I ever hurt you in any way." He looked embarrassed as his eyes flickered from my face towards the window and back again.

"You are the most special girl I have ever met, and I want you to be the most important person in my life."

I blushed as he spoke. My head was spinning at the rapid change in direction of our conversation.

"I don't want to rush you into anything you don't want. I'm not out to use you and I'm not after one thing. Let me reassure you, that's not what I'm about."

I was beginning to realise this now. I felt totally relaxed, comfortable and safe. Safe with a guy who was actually interested in me! This thought made me even more excited than ever. Ashley was beginning to mean so much...perhaps *too* much, to me, but as long as his promise held out that he would never hurt me, I would be all right. I held on to that thought, as we held each other tight.

Hearing the sound of car tyres scrunching on gravel, Ashley and I looked at each other with surprise.

"I'm sure they said they'd be out all day. Sorry, I know you wanted us to be alone today. I'll see who it is. Wait here."

My heart sank as I heard several voices in the hall, all loud and seemingly all talking at once. I should have known that very private moment was just too good to last.

❧ Nine ❦

The family was home early. I cringed at the thought of having to be introduced and then explaining my disability. I was always embarrassed at meeting new people, afraid I was going to overbalance or trip over something.

Why did I always have to think of such things? Mum said I should have been in a wheelchair by the time I was ten, but I had defied all the doctors. No way was I going to be stuck in a chair. Who would marry someone in a wheelchair? Wheelchair users were seen as victims. I was not a victim and I would not use a wheelchair.

Ashley walked back in ahead of the crowd.

"It's okay," he said softly. "I've explained all. Just be yourself. You don't have to prove yourself to them, or to anyone, right?"

I thought he looked like a fashion model standing there, so perfectly handsome.

"Did you hear?"

I managed a nod. "Mmm."

"You're not worried are you?"

"Of course not," I lied, vaguely wondering if I would go to hell for the untruth.

"Don't worry," he whispered. "My family will love you."

"I'm not afraid of them, just that I'll make a fool of myself," I explained. "And they may not like me. Don't you think they'll be surprised at you bringing someone ... like me ... home with you?"

"What do you mean *like you*? Don't put yourself down. You just have a nice wiggle!" Ashley grinned as he said this and gave me a wicked wink. Then he slid his arms round my waist and drew me blissfully close to him. "Look, they already know. We don't have any secrets in our family. Mum has always taught us to be open about our feelings; it saves a lot of grief later on if we have problems at school or anything." He grinned at me. "I've told them you're a friend, but they will no doubt read more into that."

I tried not to blush. "Er, as you are embracing me like a girlfriend, isn't that what they *will* think I am, anyway?" It was meant as a joke, but I soon wished I had kept quiet.

"Is that what you want to be, then? My girlfriend?" He was laughing.

"What's so funny?" I said, indignantly.

"Oh," he said, sharply. "I'm not laughing about you wanting to be my girlfriend. Here's my response to that!"

With that, he pulled me into a clinch and kissed me, probing and teasing with his tongue. And that was his family's first glimpse of me as they all entered the room together. Oh, my God! My head was spinning. I was deliriously happy. But what must they have thought, coming home and finding us like that?

The kissing was interrupted by exaggerated coughing and girly tittering.

"Ahem. Hi, Orianna, I'm Philippa, Ashley's older sister."

Small and pixie-like, Philippa bounced enthusiastically towards me. She was exquisite – everything I wished that I could be, very petite at about 4ft 10in with long dark hair, and graceful agility.

"I hope we will be great friends," she said, taking my arm. "Anyone who makes Ashley happy must be special."

She hugged me like an old friend. I liked her. She was open and genuine, and for that reason alone, I knew we could be friends.

Next came his brothers. Jon, the older one, just smiled and said, "Hi." He was about 24 and seemed charming and polite. He looked like an older version of Ashley and was just as good looking. Ashley had described Jon as their protective older brother.

Then the younger brother came in. He stared at me for a second but when I smiled back, he grinned at me and plonked himself down on the sofa, watching his family interact as they came in the room… Joshua must have been about 12, fresh faced, with green eyes and a broad smile.

Finally, his parents appeared. I needn't have worried. They were all smiles and made me feel welcome.

"Nice to meet you, Orianna, I'm Rose. We have heard such good things about you!" Ashley's mum beamed, coming forward to embrace me.

Rose was in her late forties and very classically dressed. She looked as if she had just stepped off the cover of a 1950's edition of *Vogue*. She reminded me of a starlet from the old Hollywood era. She was classy and well spoken, like an English version of Dita Von Teese. Rose had the same startling blue eyes as Ashley.

She slid a CD into the music system and David Oistrakh's rendition of *Clair de Lune* floated through the speakers.

"That is magical music, very French," she enthused. "What a great composer Debussy was."

"And we have heard what a great artist *you* are too," Ashley's dad said to me.

Stephen Mason was every bit as good looking as everyone else in the family. It was sickening. They obviously had good genes. Stephen stood about 6ft, was dark-haired with green eyes and had the same chiselled features as Ashley and Jon.

I didn't know what to say to these people whom I had only just met, but who were making me feel so special. I blushed, feeling quite emotional, and Ashley squeezed my arm in a gesture of support.

As they all sat down we settled into easy conversation, as if I had known them for years, talking about all sorts of stuff. I was telling Rose about my fashion course and the bodices we were working on.

"I have some original garments from my great-great grandmother's era," she said. There's a huge trunk in the loft packed with corsets and her wedding dress, as well as shoes. When you come over another time I'll get it all out for you. I'm sure it will inspire your studies."

"That would be wonderful. Thank you ever so much." I was blushing again because of her kindness. Now I was falling in love with the family.

Ashley put his arm around me, apparently very happy for me to be there. I don't think Rose would have cared if I'd had green hair, talked gobbledegook, had webbed feet or a third eye. She obviously wanted someone unpretentious to love her son for who he was as a person and not because of his family connections. It was encouraging that she seemed to think I would be "good" for Ashley.

"So what do you hope to do when you finish sixth form?" Stephen asked.

"Art. Well, fine art."

He smiled. "Any ideas where you would like to go?"

"London, I think. If I had the opportunity, I'd like to go to St Martin's or The Royal College of Art, but I'm not sure I'm good enough to go there."

"Don't underestimate yourself," Rose intervened. "I think if your tutor helps you to prepare your portfolio, you will have no trouble getting in there."

"Mum, Anna's work is amazing – it's far better than mine," Ashley said.

I began to fidget in my chair, feeling uncomfortable to be receiving so much praise.

Ashley noticed. "You are an incredible artist, Anna, you need to realise that."

I squeezed his hand, thanking him for his generous words.

"Let's get some tea, Anna." Rose ushered me off the sofa, steering me by my elbow towards the kitchen.

Leaning against the work unit, waiting for the kettle to boil, Rose handed me a Chinese takeaway menu.

"Do you like Chinese food, Anna?"

"Yes, I do, very much." I tried not to think about the sandwiches Ashley and I had devoured earlier. The fresh air from the morning had made me hungry, and we had eaten everything he had made between us. My tummy wasn't capable of rumbling at the thought of more food.

"There's a takeaway in the next village – we can order for everyone and they'll deliver." She smiled. "Is there anything that you particularly like?"

"I love all Chinese food. But Ashley and I had sandwiches together earlier, I'm not sure I'd be able to eat anything else right now. ," I laughed.

"I noticed the dirty plates on the side. You don't have to eat if you aren't hungry. We all love Chinese, and you want to stay you are most welcome. I'm so glad you feel comfortable with us."

Ashley's mum made the tea, and then phoned the order for the Chinese take-out, confidently reeling the numbers off the menu to the member of staff at the other end.

Philippa came into the kitchen. "I'll do that, Mum, you go and relax."

Rose and I went into the little side room where Ashley and I had sat for the entire afternoon. She sat beside me and started a conversation.

"I wanted to let you know, Anna … may I call you Anna?"

"Yes, please do, I prefer it."

"I wanted to say that Ashley has completely come out of himself since he's met you. I don't think you realise how good you are for him. He misses his friends in London, naturally, and, well, between you and me, Nathan isn't exactly the kind of boy we like Ashley hanging around with."

There was concern in her voice. What could I say?

"Oh, right." I just continued listening.

"We have learnt things about Nathan Cooper that we just don't like." She hesitated for a moment before asking, "How do you feel about Nathan?"

"Um, well, he's not exactly popular. His reputation isn't good. He easily influences others. Let's put it this way, he is feared rather than liked at school."

When Philippa came in with the tea I was frowning. "Sorry," I said, "I can't think of anything likeable about him."

Philippa smiled. "It's okay, Orianna – Mum's hoping your *friendship* with Ashley will distract him from hanging around with Nathan, that's all."

I laughed to myself at the way Philippa expressed the word "friendship", adding huge connotations to it.

Philippa gave me a puzzled look, not realising she'd made a joke.

"Let's forget about Nathan," Rose said. "I just want to say that we are really pleased Ashley has met you."

So I was officially a "hit" with the Masons. I wondered why. They must have seen something in me that endeared me to them? Blushing again with embarrassment, I just smiled back politely, not knowing quite what to say. Everyone was relaxed; it was that kind of house. Rose, Philippa and I were drinking tea as we chatted; Joshua was in the entertainment room on his games console, while Jon, Ashley and their dad were flicking through car magazines, discussing the pros and cons of the latest Porsche models

When the door bell rang, Rose went to answer it, expecting the food delivery. It wasn't. She came back into the room looking rather upset, the reason for her disquiet following at her heels. It was a friend of Ashley's... none other than Nathan. He stopped just inside the doorway, looking sheepish, while Rose went to call Ashley.

As soon as he spotted me in the room, he stared at me, eyes narrowed, in a threatening way.

I tried not to visibly squirm and averted my gaze.

"Hi, Nathan. What can I do for you?" Ashley asked politely.

"Uh, I just dropped this CD by that I borrowed. I thought you'd want it back. You off out to Bournemouth tonight? A few of us are meeting up at Yates's bar, fancy it?"

"No, not tonight, Nathan. I'm busy," Ashley insisted.

Nathan shot a sideways glare at me, obviously wishing in that moment that I didn't exist.

"Okay, then. Whatever." He shrugged his shoulders and pulled his face into an ugly grimace.

Ashley saw him out and after five minutes or so, returned to his family and me. The tense atmosphere that had crept in with Nathan disappeared; the food eventually arrived and we had a lovely evening. I was so comfortable there, it felt like a second skin and I didn't want to leave. My presence here had obviously not gone down well with Nathan, though. I knew he hated me, and seeing him again at school would prove the intensity of his feelings towards me.

My walking felt easier, lighter, as I almost danced through the school corridors. The sunlight, through the window panes, jived across my skin, making me feel even more radiant. I wore a huge grin on my face for most of the morning... until I saw Nathan. His gimlet eyes stared at me repulsively across the corridor. So he hadn't taken my acquaintance with Ashley at all well. No surprises there, but it didn't matter. I quickly flicked my gaze away from him. He wasn't even worth looking at. Immersed in my thoughts as I continued in the opposite direction to Nathan, I suddenly found myself in collision with a fellow student.

"Sorry, I—" A pair of strong, yet gentle hands saved me from sprawling full length. I allowed myself to be steadied by them and again felt that tingle of pleasure when I saw who they belonged to.

"Oh! Ash…ley, it's you!" I sounded like Scarlett O'Hara in *Gone With The Wind*; the heroine dreaming of being embraced by her hero.

"Hello, Anna. Please let me introduce myself. My name's Mason, Ashley Mason!" His grip on my shoulders prevented my feet from slipping out from under me, as I collided with him.

"Stop being silly!"

"I'm only having fun!" His face beamed as his gaze met mine.

"I know. How are you today?"

"Better for seeing you!"

My face flushed crimson. "Oh, by the way, I meant to say…I'm picking up my new car tomorrow. Would you come with Amelia and me to collect it? We could go for a spin, perhaps – have lunch in a pub? What do you think?"

"Great. Yeah, I'd love that. Let me pick you both up from yours, then? What time?"

"Say about 10.45. I have to collect the car at 11.30 from the dealer's, and then we can go from there."

People were shoving past us in the corridor.

I could feel Ashley's arm curved around my shoulders as he tried to protect me from the chattering throng of students hurrying past. His embrace warmed me; I felt calm, safe.

"I must go, babe." He raised his hand hesitantly, conflict showing briefly in his eyes, as if he didn't want to leave me and then he lightly caressed my cheekbone with his fingertips. His skin was warm and the trail his fingers left on my cheek gave me a strange, intense glow. He walked away, presumably to his next class.

As I turned to say goodbye, his face surprised me. His expression seemed torn, almost in pain, and so amazingly beautiful, that the aching inside me to be close to him was stronger than ever. My "goodbye" stuck in my throat as I watched him disappear down the corridor.

Ashley was at my door on time the next day, looking as delicious as ever. The sky was quite overcast, but that didn't matter because as soon as I set eyes on him the sun was shining in my world.

"We'll go in my car, Amelia, if that's okay?" Ashley smiled at Amelia, almost having the same effect on her as he did on me.

"Yeah, cool," she replied, doing her coat up as we left my house. Ashley walked close beside me to the car door; I could feel his hand in the small of my back as he did his gentlemanly thing. I sighed, thinking how lovely it was to have such a caring boyfriend. He seemed to read my thoughts as he gave me a quizzical glance. He held the passenger door open for me to get in, closing it gently behind me.

We pulled out of our side road and Ashley eased the car into the traffic, using his satnav to direct us to the dealer's showroom. He was paying attention to the road, occasionally viewing me sideways as if to check I was still there. Amelia babbled away in embarrassment from the back seat; maybe she felt like a gooseberry.

Ashley smiled in my direction. He was driving fast, ignoring traffic signs.

"You should slow down; you'll get done by a speed camera!" Amelia called to him.

He grinned at her in the rear view mirror. "Hey, I'm a teenager. Aren't we supposed to drive fast?"

"You're going nearly 45 in a 30 zone!" I shouted above the stereo. The pavements were busy with dog walkers, mums with buggies and the elderly dragging shopping trolleys, dithering over which direction to go in.

He rolled his eyes. "Relax, Anna. I've never been caught."

"Are you trying to kill us all?" Amelia demanded.

"No, of course not!" Ashley laughed. "We're not going to crash!"

"Why are you driving so fast?" I demanded to know.

"You want to get your car don't you?" He found it all very amusing.

"Yeah, I do. Like, that's my *point*, right?"

The dealership building, all glass and glossy black framework, looked modern and fresh against the milky sky. Ashley pulled into a free space directly in front of the Mini section of the showroom. A couple of sales guys were standing around sipping coffee, waiting for non-existent customers during the credit crunch. The R8's roaring engine was silenced by the turn of a key and three seat belts simultaneously clicked out of their restraints.

Entering the showroom, I could smell that heady "new car" mixture of adhesive and polished metal, plastic, virgin rubber tyres and the sexiest of all – leather upholstery. With the fresh, crisp smell of precision engineering in my nostrils, I stepped confidently towards the sales team as they huddled together in a group.

Fake smiles greeted me.

"Can we help you, miss?" One stepped out of the coven, pushing his ill-fitting glasses back on the bridge of his nose.

"My girlfriend has come to pick up her motability vehicle," Ashley informed him, using his "I'm in control" tone.

Perhaps because Ashley and Amelia were there to provide support, I felt emboldened, and able to handle this myself.

"My name is Orianna Stewart," I asserted.

"Oh, right."

The sales guy seemed shocked when he realised the mini was intended for me. He obviously thought I was too young to afford a car such as this. The cheek of it – what did he know?

As I watched the new pink mini emerge from the adjoining garage holding area , I appreciated how privileged I was to get a new car on the scheme. I was allowed to choose a brand new car from the list every three years. Until now, Mum had just collected the allowance, but now that I had passed my test she decided to use the money for me to choose a brand new car.

I had scrolled down the scheme's list of vehicles on the internet, trying to decide on the car I wanted. I had been to loads of dealerships and test driven a few cars, but my decision had been made, and I chose a brand new, second generation, automatic Mini convertible.

I saw Ashley beaming at me as I sat in the driving seat amidst the champagne sparkling pink interior. Even though it was winter, I flicked the switch to roll back the roof. As it lowered, I felt the cool air around me.

"It's a bit cold for that yet!" Amelia laughed.

Ivory leather seats caressed me as I sank my shoes into the plush pink carpet of the footwell. Decadent, maybe, but it fitted my style perfectly. I'd had to pay more for the designer extras, but I didn't care; it was exactly the specification of Mini I wanted.

Gloating now, I realised I would never have to drive that rather ordinary Nissan Micra ever again. I had hated it and had already sent it back to the dealership. It had been an uncool choice by my mother, especially for someone of my age.

"Don't you look the part, babe?" Ashley said, apparently happy to be sharing my joy.

Amelia poked her head inside. "Wow! Now everyone's going to be sooooo jealous of you! Wait till Jess clocks it, pink is her colour."

"Can I have a try?" Ashley asked. He was just like a kid with a new toy and his eyes sparkled like sapphires as he checked out the dashboard and CD system.

"It's not my colour. But the stereo is almost as good as mine!" He nodded, giving me a double thumbs-up of approval.

"Let's get the paperwork signed and sealed, and then we can head off for a drive," I suggested.

"Cool." Amelia agreed.

"I'll go with Amelia and grab us some fish and chips while you do the necessary. We won't be long." Ashley added. I signed the required paperwork, paid the deposit and waited for the garage to do its final checks on the car. We all decided to sit in Ashley's car in the dealership carpark, sharing the chips so that my lovely new car didn't end up stinking with the smell of strong vinegar. I hurriedly ate what I wanted, so that I could take my new car out for a spin.

Windows down, I could feel the wind in my hair as Amelia and I made for Bournemouth. We could hear Ashley's voice through the speakers as the Bluetooth technology kicked in.

"Can you see me following behind? What's the reception like with your phone? You look like 'it' girls in that car!" I could hear him laughing.

"He's having more fun than me!" I giggled.

"Yeah, but this car is so amazing," Amelia enthused. You are sooooo lucky. I can't wait till the kids at school see this. The guys will be falling over themselves for you!"

"I think not! She's off the market, I hope."

Amelia and I fell into fits of giggles as we realised Ashley was still live on the Bluetooth.

"I don't think Amelia intended for you to hear that," I replied.

"Amelia, close your ears, please," Ashley instructed. "Anna, you are my life – remember that."

I fell silent at that remark, which seemed quite full on. I hoped our friendship wasn't moving too fast. I didn't want it to fail.

❧ Ten ❧

Later that night, I dreamt again of Ashley Mason. The majority of girls at school probably had at some time or another. They would have picked this guy out of the crowd because of his masculine build with just the right amount of muscle, and those unforgettable eyes. Strong and self-assured, he was no skinny geek. In fact, he could easily pass for a Hollywood movie star. Okay, I was biased, but it was the truth anyway. I knew my thoughts continually gushed about him, yet I couldn't help myself. Sometimes he was so cute, exactly like the guys in the movies. If any man other than Ashley talked to me that way, I would burst out laughing, but when flattering and flirty words left Ashley's lips, they sounded utterly delicious.

And those artistic skills…most girls would die for the opportunity of having their portrait sketched by him. Definitely some gold stars to be picked up there. His manners were impeccable but understated, being part of his natural make up. Girls did not often encounter this respectfulness. Sure, he was protective and looked out for me because of my disability, but true gentlemen have always appealed to girls as a reinforcement of their femininity and their innate need to feel protected. Ashley could have a face like a truck, and still the girls would consider him to be "so friggin' hot and sexy" because of the way he treated them. Ashley was the dream that made women's hearts flutter at the thought of having a man who respected them, put them first, and was gentle in the way he walked beside her through life. He was my dream.

Every school up and down the country had one – an "it" crowd. These were the pupils who thought they were special for some particular reason. The sort of teenagers in this category that came to mind were those depicted in teen films, such as *Mean Girls* and the modern version of *Dangerous Liaisons* called *Cruel Intentions*. Wimborne Upper School was no exception and we did not escape from having these particular "types" of students. They were the ones who were spoilt. Their parents owned flash, expensive cars. They wore the latest designer clothes, used the latest mobile phones and hung out in the smarter parts of town. Most, especially the girls, spent their weekends shopping at West Quay in Southampton or Richmond Classics in Bournemouth. A new pair of jeans may set them back anything from £90 upwards; but their clothes had to be the hottest designer labels and up-to-the-minute in style.

I didn't resent their lifestyles; I just thought it was ridiculous for kids of our age to be like that. Perhaps they were trying to grow up too fast, especially the girls. They were all over made up, with hair extensions, diamanté "bling" jewellery and the latest Louis Vuitton handbags. Their skirts were more like belts and when the wind blew, left nothing to the boys' imaginations! Behind their backs, these girls were ridiculed for looking and acting so above themselves.

There was, of course, their hardened fan base that tried to emulate them, albeit rather badly, mainly because of the lack of funds. Jessica fell into this category, a fact of which I often reminded her, but she never took the hint or tried to change her style. It was how she was and I couldn't dislike her for it.

Nathan Cooper's new girlfriend, Aimee, was an "it" girl and really thought she was *it*. You could smell her sickly designer fragrance before you actually saw her. She was normally surrounded by her posse, or fan base. It was an amusing sight. She always wore baby pink, with some kind of designer logo emblazoned on a hoodie, or on her shoes or handbags. The shoes were something to behold. They were black or pink, with heels of five to six inches in height, and satin bows or diamanté "bling" buckles. Surely they were not Manolo Blahnik? But they certainly looked like it. Aimee could hardly walk in them, which actually made me laugh…was she trying to impersonate me? Ha ha, that would be the day!

She had once made my life hell. Bullying people less fortunate than herself was her forte. Special needs kids were an easy target, not that I had been classed as having special educational needs, but my physical problems had labelled me as one and she had targeted me a lot. Every lunchtime was the same. She and her little gang of followers would form a semi-circle around me, backing me up against a wall. I was always alone. One time Aimee did this knowing that I couldn't run away or escape. The task of the day was to humiliate me in some way, so she decided to get Nathan Cooper, who was just a classmate at the time, and not her boyfriend, to hold me against a wall whilst she smeared all my make-up over my face with a facial wipe. Then she reapplied my make-up in her own unique way. This involved using the most garish-coloured eye shadows applied in the most childlike, clownish manner you could imagine. Face painting with venom! When she had finished, I would look like Morticia from *The Addams Family*. The end result would leave everyone creased up with laughter.

"So you think you look pretty now?" She'd taunt. "Well, do you? Look in the mirror," she'd screech, pulling a compact from her bag and thrusting it into my face so that I could see her handiwork.

It was degrading with everyone watching and that was exactly how she had intended it to be. I had never forgotten those incidents. She was an utter cow. Everyone knew how cruel and mean she could be, yet she still had her faithful followers. From that time on, I vowed that I would never be like her and would rise above that sort of behaviour.

However, now there was a problem. She was part of the "it" crowd that Ashley and Nathan belonged to. Fortunately, Ashley wasn't at the school at the time of those subjections made by his peers and I was relieved. But how would Nathan and Aimee react when they realised that Ashley was seeing me? It was best not to think about it; I would rise above it, try to be better than them, a better person inside. If I couldn't look perfect on the surface, I'd damned well try to be as good as possible within my skin. Maybe one day I would win them over; I just didn't know how I was going to do that.

Then I wondered whether Ashley had already spoken to Nathan and Aimee. Something had changed their attitude towards me and it was weird. Walking through the corridors with Jessica, Jack and Amelia on the way to class; Nathan nodded and grunted at me as he passed. Aimee, however, was positively gushing.

Grabbing both my hands, she said, "You must come and sit with us at lunch, if you are meeting Ashley."

From then on, that's how it was; they treated me as if I was best friends with them all. I was still sceptical, but endured their effusion for Ashley's sake. The "friendship" with the "it" crowd seemed to be developing at an incredulous rate. I didn't know for whose sake it was – theirs, Ashley's or mine – but then decided it couldn't possibly be mine! I would go with the flow and see where it led; be open to possibilities. I always looked for the best in people, and there must have been something "okay" about this group of people for Ashley to be friends with them.

Amelia, Jess and I were having lunch one day when Nathan and Aimee suddenly decided to join us. The three of us sat there looking at each other, open-mouthed, as they sat down.

"To what do we owe this honour?" Jess said sarcastically.

Stay objective, stay indifferent, I told myself.

"We haven't always seen eye to eye?" Aimee directed her question at me, with a confident stare.

I was the only one who could see through her, and she knew it. Well, I would play along, for Ashley's sake.

"I would agree with you." I gave her a false smile. Aimee didn't deserve loyalty from me because of how she had treated me in the past.

Nathan was just as fake, fawning over Amelia and Jess, especially Jess. He knew how much she fancied him. I couldn't think why. He was so vile. Aimee was welcome to him. I was glad he didn't have any of my friends in his clutches.

I could feel Nathan's eyes boring into me. Why did he always have to stare at me like that? When Ashley came across and sat down beside me it was even worse.

Amelia and Jess began nudging each other, grinning and winking at me. Hoping no one could hear, I hissed, "Stop it!" between my teeth.

I became hyper-aware of Ashley sitting only an inch away from me and was stunned by the unexpected surge of electricity that arose between us. I felt an almost overwhelming urge to reach out and stroke his god-like face. Definitely not advisable in the present company. I balled my hands tightly into fists and kept them on my lap out of harm's way until Ashley's warm hand crept beneath the table towards mine in a mirrored demonstration of my thoughts. My hand interlocked with his. No one else could see. The pulse between us was like a drug, a fix – something neither of us seemed to be able to control. It felt amazing to me, and there was more to it than sexual attraction alone.

Was I in love? I felt as if I was losing my mind. Ashley peered sideways at me. I smiled sheepishly as I realised his body language and eye contact was identical to mine. Was he in love with me? He had said he liked my mind – well, everything about me, including my crap legs. Wow…what a guy! He was almost the perfect fictional character, except this guy was real!

Ashley's gaze flitted from face to face as everyone exchanged comments. Although he was grinning as he gripped my hand ever tighter, his eyes still managed to smoulder, even under the cafeteria's harsh fluorescent lights. I looked away before anyone realised what was happening. I was hyper-ventilating. God, it was completely ridiculous that I felt so high.

Lunch break seemed very short, but I wanted to savour every moment. I didn't try to concentrate on the conversation; it was impossible. I couldn't even think about the subjects they were discussing. I tried unsuccessfully to relax, but the highly charged current passing between us never loosened its grip.

Occasionally I would permit myself a fleeting glance in his direction, but Ashley didn't seem to relax, either. His lips were tightly sealed and he was quiet, apart from the odd stifled snigger directed at the pretentiousness of his friends. My fingers, tightly intertwined with his, were throbbing with the delight of their new hiding place.

Then the bell rang, signalling the end of lunch. Was it my imagination, or did it sound sharper, more insistent than usual? I breathed a sigh of regret as Ashley's hand reluctantly parted company with mine.

So here I was, a few days later, on my way to a party at the ringleader's house. I had no idea what to expect, but as Ashley was with me, I felt safe entering this unknown den of iniquity. Well, at least that was how I saw it. The house was nowhere near as inviting as Ashley's family home, but I would tolerate the party this evening for Ashley's sake.

The house was just off the square in Wimborne, next to the pub. On the outside it was painted cream, with ivy trailing around the windows and front door. Black wrought iron railings enclosed the front garden of the house, which faced directly onto a main one-way street, leading to the square.

Ashley had parked the R8 in the car park belonging to the pub. As we walked along the street, I saw other sixth formers and some year-11 girls entering the house. Before we even reached the front door, we could feel as well as hear loud music rhythmically thump-thumping out into the cool night air. I thought it was some alternative Brit rock or pop playing. If Nathan kept the music at that volume, he was likely to be cautioned by the police for noise pollution. Anyway, it was his house and his responsibility.

We went into a large entrance hall with a long, winding staircase, rather like those portrayed in old black and white movies on a Saturday afternoon. There were bodies everywhere; sitting on stairs, leaning against walls, lying on the floor and perching on stools or any available seats. Most had drinks in their hands, some smoked cigarettes and a few were obviously smoking something that they shouldn't have been.

Some couples were sucking face and a few were groping each other a little too much for a public place. It made me feel very uncomfortable and Ashley realised that from the look on my face.

"I'll find us somewhere quiet to sit. Would that be better?"

"That would be lovely," I agreed. With that, we headed off in the direction of one of the lounges. Nathan was there, sitting amongst his audience and the blonde bimbo, Aimee, was sprawled on the arm of the sofa, next to Nathan, with her cleavage well on show. The air was heavy with fag smoke, alcopops and cider.

"Hey, Ashley, mate! Glad you could make it." He got up from where he was holding court, shrugged the "it" girl off his arm in a nonchalant way, and grabbed Ashley in a man-hug. He looked in my direction, just about managing to acknowledge me with a nod and a hello. I was still not sure whether he accepted Ashley and me or not. Only time would tell, but it really didn't matter as Ashley was the only one who was important to me here.

"Hey Ashley, fancy something a bit stronger than cider? There's some vodka upstairs. Let's go up and try that. Come on, Orianna, I'm sure you would like some?"

"Well, yes, okay. A small glass wouldn't hurt." I replied. I had never tried vodka, so to avoid looking stupid, I accepted the invitation. I had to live a little. I would sip it very slowly. I was nearly legally allowed to drink. It really wouldn't hurt. I had always played it safe and been told I needed to lighten up a bit. Perhaps now was a good time to try.

"I'm with you. You'll be fine." Ashley tried to reassure me.

We followed Nathan, the bimbo and two more couples upstairs to Nathan's room. His room was painted bright red and his choice of furniture was black, glossy, masculine style with minimalist Japanese themes going on. A large, black four-poster bed dominated the centre of the room. It had black drapes and was made up with black silk sheets. Aimee hauled herself onto the bed, lounging on it like she owned it.

Nathan produced the alcohol and about a dozen glasses. Playing the generous host, he poured a glass for everyone, giving me the fullest glass of all. I definitely wasn't going to drink it all, but I took it from him anyway. He gave me a sly wink as I took a small sip. I decided that I would try to avoid him as much as I could. I still felt uneasy about him; a little afraid even, but I would never let him know that.

His bimbo was the first to feel the effects of the alcohol. A little while later, she was drunk and pawing all over Nathan, which he hated. Public signs of affection or allegiance from a woman were not his passion. Everyone else was chatting or dancing to a CD and were generally having fun.

Ashley and I sat together, arms entwined, just chatting, about art, politics, fashion music and film – all our usual topics of conversation. We never put on any airs and graces with each other; we were happy just being ourselves. We fitted together as a couple just like pieces in a jigsaw puzzle, and the emotional and physical intensity between us was something that continued growing.

Nathan sat on the other side of the sofa, oblivious to everyone as he poured some white powder out onto his black lacquered coffee table and began to chop it with a debit card. Ashley suddenly rose from his seat.

"If you are going to do that rubbish and be some kind of junkie, I'm out of here!" he shouted. With that, he helped me out of my seat and guided me to the door, anxious to escape Nathan's perverse and unlawful idea of fun. We trailed off downstairs, meandering through the hordes of sweaty, intoxicated dancers and socialites, to an open space in the garden. We found a bench under a honeysuckle and held each other, gazing up at the clear night sky that twinkled with stars.

"Why is Nathan like that? He is such a prat," I scoffed.

Ashley couldn't help but laugh. "He's his own worst enemy. Nothing can stop him doing what he wants. His pathetic, crazy, pastimes will get him into a great deal of trouble one day."

"You really shouldn't have anything more to do with him," I said. "He's trouble. You are far better than him. He doesn't deserve you as a friend, you know that."

"I will do something about it soon, I promise, when it's the right time. I've known him a long time. So out of respect, I want to talk to him when I know he will take on board what I tell him."

"Respect? He doesn't deserve your respect! He's a low-life! I know you could have friends with far higher morals than him."

Ashley pulled me closer. I snuggled up against his chest, listening to his pounding heart. I absorbed his fragrance, still overwhelmed by the intensity between us. He was an incredible person and always would be, to me. In that moment I realised just how lucky I was to have found him and I really believed I was the luckiest woman alive.

As we sat in the darkness, I began to feel the cool breeze dancing around me, and shivered. Ashley drew me as close to him as he could.

"Do you want your coat? Where is it?"

"I think I left it up in Nathan's room. I'll pop back and get it, if you want to go and fetch the car? Do you fancy popping into Amelia's for a coffee on the way back?" I suggested.

"Yes, that would be nice. Not too late is it?"

"She stays up late at weekends. But her mum never minds people dropping in."

"As long as you're sure?"

"Positive," I assured him. "I'll get my coat and meet you at the car in a few minutes." I kissed him hard on the lips, leaving him wanting more.

"I love you, sexy!" he said with a grin.

I tried to replicate his grin seductively, but failed miserably. I think he just said he loved me. I wasn't sure I'd heard right.

"Stop teasing me, babe," I replied. "But you should know, you are everything to me."

Ashley grabbed my hand and pulled me close to his firm body.

"Well, miss, you are mine now. Nothing else but you matters to me. I bet I love you more than you love me!"

Before I could answer, Ashley's lips were pressed impatiently against mine and all I could think of was whether he could taste the remnants of my lip gloss and I hoped my breath smelt okay! Then I began to melt on the spot as he wrapped his muscular arms around me. As we kissed, he held my face in both hands. This was his first attempt at being passionate with me, and so far I'd deduced that he knew what to do and say when the mood was right.

His tongue prized my lips apart. I couldn't resist him and reciprocated the move. We were full on kissing now. The taste of him was like strawberries, refreshing, succulent and sweet. His hands travelled down my back, caressing me as he drew me close, finally coming to rest in the small of my back. My whole body tingled as waves of emotion and passion were awoken within me. I had this overwhelming desire to give myself to him, but I wanted to wait and hoped he would want to wait, too. As if reading my thoughts, he released me from his embrace and walked away, out of the garden, towards the car park and into the darkness.

Reluctantly letting go of him, I walked in the opposite direction, towards Nathan's front door to get my coat. Swarms of teenagers still filled the house which reeked of smoke, drugs and booze and was littered with the shattered dreams of those hoping to find soulmates. We had all been sold the lie by books and movies that the "happy ending" fairytale was available for everyone to take.

I opened Nathan's bedroom door and walked in. I wanted to get back to Ashley as quickly as possible, not wanting to miss a moment with him, especially now I knew how he felt about me.

The room was almost in darkness. I could see nothing. It was creepy. I fumbled around for the light switch, just wanting to find my coat and get out of there. Suddenly, I realised I was not alone. Nathan was slouched in a chair. He looked as if he was dead.

"Nathan, are you okay?" I shook his arm to see if he was alive. He grunted and looked up, shocked to see me there.

"What are you doing back here?" He hissed the question through his teeth, lumbering clumsily to his feet.

"I've come back to get my coat. Do you know where it is?"

"Haven't seen it." He moved in closer to me, backing me up against his bedroom door. What the hell did he think he was doing? Before I realised it, his arm was behind my back, and I heard the key turn sharply as he locked me in his room. What was he thinking? To avoid a confrontation, I thought it best to humour him for a few minutes, find my coat, and then I would go. I stood rigidly in front of him, not quite knowing what to do or where to look.

"So what's with you and my mate Ashley, then? Are you giving it to him? Are you an easy lay? It has to be the only reason why Ashley would be interested in someone like *you*!" Nathan obviously hadn't changed at all; he was still rude, lewd and impossibly arrogant.

There was no mistaking the venom in his tone. "That isn't it at all!" I yelled. "Not that it's any of *your* business." This was not a conversation I wanted to have with him at all.

"Well, you are quite pretty, I suppose," he said, lifting my chin between his fingers and thumb as if to examine my features. He contemplated my face for a moment, then, with no warning he hooked my elbows in his hands, guiding me away from the door.

"Come here," he said, motioning me with his eyes to the bed. "Talk to me … let me get to know you, uh? If Ashley thinks you're special then you must have something."

I was reluctant. But if I went for the door, then I knew he would beat me to it and force me to stay. There was no use me trying to run; I couldn't. I wouldn't be able to get away and my screams for help would never be heard above the music thudding out downstairs. Okay, I would chat with him for five minutes … try to be nice, then find my coat and be gone.

I sat on the very edge of his bed, frozen to the spot like a statue waiting to come alive.

"Don't be shy. Let me be your friend." His arm slithered around me, but I wasn't convinced by his sudden show of affection. He rubbed his hand up and down my back. I tried to shrug him off but it wasn't working. He leaned in towards me, invading my space. He flicked my hair back off my face with his fingers and I gagged as I caught a whiff of his stinking breath.

Ugh…fags and stale booze and God knew what else. Gripping both of my shoulders, he turned me to face him. I tried not to look shocked; if I did it might encourage him even more.

"Come on, one kiss won't hurt. Are you frigid?" He was persistent now.

"No! I don't want to kiss you, now let me go!" I was raising my voice, but it wasn't loud enough to attract anyone else's attention.

Insistently, he pushed me back onto the bed. If that was his idea of being friendly, I didn't want to know how he treated his enemies.

"Look, I just want to spend some time alone with you. Don't moan. A girl like you doesn't get an offer like this every day, you know. Just go with it, enjoy it." He was annoyed now, because I wasn't complying with what he wanted. His face was all screwed up and twisted with fury as he bore down on me.

Then it dawned on me that he was going to hurt me. I couldn't get away. His body weight on top of me was far too heavy. His frame was bigger, much stronger, and he was persistent. By now he had one hand clamped firmly over my mouth. I felt suffocated and not in control. Now I realised how naïve I was about men. He straddled me. With his free hand he was tearing at my clothes. I struggled, trying to resist him, but he was far too strong for me to fight against.

"If you try to scream or struggle, I'll kill you."

I had been trying to scream, but no sound would come out. My chest felt tight, as if I couldn't get any air into my lungs. I could still smell his repulsive breath and his hands were pawing roughly at my exposed body. I felt nauseous and wanted to scream but I was helpless. I desperately tried to move, to break free, but it was no use.

"Why don't you make this easy for me? Open your legs!" he snarled.

"Okay, bitch, let's get this over with!" My face stung as he slapped me hard a few times, hoping it would make me compliant. Tears welled up in my eyes as I realised I would have to go through with this ordeal; there was just no way of getting away from him. I was mortified and closed my eyes as tightly as I could to avoid looking at his revolting face.

"That vodka didn't loosen you up, then?"

I was trying to scream through his fingers, which were over my mouth. My body felt drained of every ounce of energy. I was exhausted from fighting. His weight just felt heavier on top of me, trapping me completely. It was my worst nightmare; I could feel his hot, sour breath on my cheek, and forced myself to keep my eyes tightly shut, not wanting to see the crazed look in his eyes. He was determined, menacing and spiteful. His drug habit had fazed him out so he had no sense of belonging to anything, apart from his recent fix. After closing my eyes and shutting out his evil face, I remembered nothing. Everything went black.

When I came to and opened my eyes, I realised I was completely naked, with a cotton sheet half-covering my exposed body. I felt sore and bruised, and ashamed.

I could hear raised voices from the en suite bathroom.

"What the hell were you doing? Answer me!" I heard a woman screech. It sounded like Aimee.

"She was begging for it," Nathan sneered. "It was the drugs; I was high...I didn't realise what I was doing." He kept his voice down, obviously not wanting anyone else overhearing their conversation.

He was a bare-faced liar. Would Aimee see through it? I winced. My body ached all over; I felt nauseous and completely drained of energy, but I knew I had to get out of there.

"Help her get fixed up, right? Make her look presentable. We don't want Ashley getting suspicious," Nathan whined. "D'you hear me?" Then he raised his voice. "For God's sake, get the bitch cleaned up! I'm out of here – I need a drink!"

"I think you've had enough!" Aimee called out as he strode past me without so much as a glance.

"Ashley's already been back in the house looking for her, wondering where she is. I gave him some excuse that I'd find her and bring him down to his car. This is the last time I support you, Nathan!" Aimee cried out, as the door slammed shut and she and I were alone. She stood in the doorway of the bathroom, one hand on her hip, shouting the odds.

"Orianna, get in here! I really don't want to know what happened. Nathan makes his own rules, but just remember this – I'm the one he always comes back to."

"You're welcome to him!" Shaking uncontrollably, I tried to dress as quickly as possible. All I wanted to do was get back to Ashley.

"I need to get back to Ashley... it must look like nothing's happened!" My voice faltered in her presence.

"Well, slut, you will need this, then." Her make up bag landed at my feet with a thud.

"I'm not helping you for your sake, but for Nathan's, so straighten yourself up and get your arse out of here!" She looked defiant and really mad, just as I remembered her from years ago, when she first started her bullying routines. I shuddered at the memories.

I could feel her staring as she watched me intently, taking in my every move.

"If you say *anything* at all to *anyone*, I promise I'll have you, so watch your back, you slut. I don't wanna set eyes on you again, got it?".

She marched out of Nathan's room as if she owned the place, and with that, she was gone.

❧ Eleven ❦

The dark embraced me. I felt strangely frozen, like a rabbit caught in headlights, in a trance. I had made my choice, although there was really no alternative, and now the time had come. This was it.

I had managed to get hold of some plastic tubing and with the aid of sharp scissors and some masking tape that I sometimes used in my art class; I had secured two lengths of the tube to the exhaust pipes of my car. Then I fed the free ends through the front windows and closed them as far as I could, stuffing two cushions into the gaps at the top. Having a twin exhaust should help to get the job over swiftly, I thought.

How could I have known when I picked the car up, just weeks ago, that it would soon be my grave? I only hoped it would be quick and painless, this way out of the mess Nathan Cooper had created.

I sat there alone in the dark with my thoughts… alone, that was, apart from that monster's baby growing inside me. Now I knew exactly what was meant by a "deafening silence". The lack of sound out there in the wilds was actually quite threatening. Was I insane to do this?

It was getting late as I sat inside my new Mini, all set up for suicide. What was I waiting for? Suddenly the wind got up, as if calling me, and began howling eerily around Knowlton Church ruins. I preferred the silence. My car already felt like a tomb, not just because of the surroundings, but also because of what I was contemplating. I knew I had to go through with it. Mixed emotions ran through my mind but what I had been considering over the last few weeks seemed to me to be the easiest solution to all my problems.

I turned the ignition key and the engine immediately sprang to life. Exhaust fumes began to fill the car. It wouldn't be too long before I lost consciousness. Death would be easy; life was harder and I couldn't face it any more. Not now, with this rape baby growing inside me. I pictured Ashley's anger if he ever found out that I'd been pregnant, and I couldn't face Mum knowing what had really happened to me, as she would blame herself. Yes, it would hurt them. I was being selfish, but they would grieve for me, and then move on with their lives. It was the best for everyone, this way. Short and sweet. Then no one would have to worry about me any more, or judge me, ridicule me, even. What a relief.

I felt very tired, and began to cough as the fumes found the back of my throat. I waited for it to take over. Soon, I would know nothing. I would just go to sleep … and never wake up. My neck felt stiff as I laid my head back against the soft leather head rest and I waited for oblivion.

Suddenly, right in front of me, I could see this amazing bright light, which was almost blinding. Was this what people meant by going towards the guiding light when you died? I waited and the light became brighter, closer and more compelling with every second. Even though I felt very woozy, I suddenly felt strong arms and heard deep voices around me. I felt as if I were being lifted and carried. So God really did have mighty angels to take you to him? How was I to know? I was a baby Christian. And as I'd never been dead before, I had no idea what to expect. Everything was hazy, but I knew the exhaust fumes had gone, so I figured I must have been on my way …

I half-opened my eyes. A light still shone, but it was now above me, and not so brilliant as before. I tried to move an arm, but something was stopping it. The realisation gradually dawned that I was still alive and conscious, lying on the back seat of a car, cocooned in a warm, thick blanket.

I was alarmed as I heard voices from the front seats. Then I recognised them. It was Ashley and his older brother, Jon.

"What do we do now?" Ashley's voice was shaky; not at all composed as it usually was.

"Well, it depends how long she was in there inhaling carbon monoxide," Jon answered.

"Shouldn't we get her to the hospital?" Ashley's voice quavered as he spoke.

"Look, Dad has a GP friend…you know, Gary. He would check her out, no questions asked." In the gloom, I saw Jon place a reassuring hand on his brother's shoulder.

But Ashley shook him off. "Why are you protecting Nathan? Orianna has attempted this because she told me Nathan had attacked her, hit her because she had a go at him about his drug taking. You know what a foul temper he has, especially when his habit takes over. I hate him, and he deserves to be punished!" Ashley sounded angry. I had never heard him like that before.

"I am not protecting Nathan at all. We can deal with him at a later date, in our own way." Jon tried again to placate Ashley. It didn't seem to be working.

My vision was still blurred but I was able to discern the knowing glance exchanged between them.

"It's his father I'm protecting," Jon argued. "He's one of Dad's closest friends. It's for the best, trust me."

Oh, God, why had it all gone wrong? I didn't want them arguing, especially over me. I wasn't worth it.

"I'll ask Amelia to stay with her overnight at our house, mainly for moral support. What do you think?" Ashley asked him.

Oh no! That was the last thing I wanted. Amelia would never understand this situation and I didn't know what kind of support she would be either.

"Good idea."

Hell! I didn't want anyone else to know what I had attempted. I was too ashamed. The conversation continued as their plans unfolded.

"If that's what you think's best," Ashley continued, "though I still think Orianna's mum should be told. And I still think she should be taken to the hospital. Surely Dad would want us to do that? We should be doing the right thing..."

I was still too choked, too dizzy, and exhausted to speak. Mum wasn't to be told! That was for definite. She would only make matters even worse... that was if they could get any worse. I even felt unsure about going to the Masons. They didn't really know me. What on earth would they think of me now? How could I tell them I was pregnant, when they were trying to help me? How could I tell Amelia, or my mum, or *anyone*? Mum would freak out. I couldn't face her. I tried not to think of the consequences of Nathan's actions. The mere mention of his name made me want to throw up. The thought of him made my skin crawl. He was disgusting; not even worth thinking about. I grappled with the thick blanket, trying to cover myself completely, trying to pretend I was still unaware of the conversation unfolding.

"I'll ring Dad straight away. I'll see if he can phone Gary and ask if he will come over tonight and check her over. Then we can all decide where to go from there."

So it was decided, without consulting me. I was hardly in a position to argue. They cared about me and it was easier to let them arrange things.

I could hear them talking on their mobiles. Their voices sounded strange and distant. Ashley talked on his hands-free system while he was driving, and I could hear Amelia's desperately worried tone through the speaker, as he relayed the plan to her. I felt too weak and disorientated to argue with them, so I let them put their scheme into practice, knowing I would be in good hands.

I remember being carried upstairs by either Jon or Ashley, into an ornate bedroom. Mrs Mason, or Rose, as she liked me to call her, and Philippa were fussing round me, trying to make sure I'd be comfortable in their surroundings. Then Amelia and Ashley tried to help, asking questions at Rose, although Ashley held back, not knowing quite how to react. I guess he disapproved about not taking me to the hospital, but he respected his dad, so went along with what was happening now.

Philippa brought me a pair of silk pyjamas and a matching dressing gown.

"Mum, Amelia and I will help Orianna change into these, and then you or Dad can send Gary straight up when he comes."

"Orianna will appreciate that," Rose said, and hugged her daughter before leading Ashley out of the room. The girls left me to wash in the en suite bathroom, helping to make me presentable after my ordeal. Neither of them said much, just smiled awkwardly at appropriate moments, when they caught my eye. Once I was tucked up in the massive four-poster bed, Gary appeared.

"Well, miss, I hear you had a very close call tonight?" He gave me the most charming smile, kind and non-judgemental.

Doctor Carlisle was very charismatic. He stood about 6ft tall, with a medium, muscular build. His face was chiselled, handsome, and almost perfect. His manner was calm, serene even. He didn't seem fazed by the predicament I had put myself in. Obviously, Ashley's dad had explained the entire situation. He did not make me feel ashamed or nervous at all. He pulled up a chair next to the bed.

"What made you try to do such a thing to yourself? I have come to check you over and make sure you are okay." His pussycat green eyes looked concerned. He brushed his fingers through his floppy blonde hair before removing some medical instruments from his case. Philippa still sat in the room on the large comfortable sofa, after suggesting I might feel more comfortable having a female present. She smiled and gave me a reassuring smile as Gary checked my breathing with his stethoscope. Lungs, heart and blood pressure were checked and he looked into my eyes with a small but bright pen torch. He said my temperature was a little high.

"Your vitals look good. Even your breathing and lungs seem okay, considering what you've been through. It looks as if Jon and Ashley reached you just in the nick of time, before any damage was done."

He looked serious. "Your temperature is definitely raised and you do look a little flushed. Do you have any other symptoms? Tell me how you are feeling?"

"Well, I feel a bit nauseous, very tired, a little dizzy and I have a headache." I was trying not to give away how I really felt.

"The headaches will hopefully pass. You need plenty of rest and lots of sleep. A mild sedative will help. I can write you a prescription for those now, and I will leave two for you to take tonight. I'd just like to take some blood and urine samples, so that we can check there is no damage to your internal organs. You really ought to be checked over by the hospital, especially your lungs. A scan would show if there has been any damage. I really recommend you to confide in your GP and your mum."

I knew he was concerned about me. The serious tone of his voice confirmed it. He gave me the sedatives, not that I wanted them. I pulled a face at the thought of taking any medication.

"One tablet will help; two would be better. Now get some rest. The Masons are very kind, they will look after you. You are in good hands." As he got up, he squeezed my hand. Then he picked up his bag and was gone.

Philippa came over to see if I was comfortable. "Orianna, we have all been so worried about you." She sat next to me on the bed. "What happened to you to make you decide to do such a thing?"

Rose came in to tidy the room and check if all was well. She looked worried and her chargin couldn't conceal her feelings.

"I'll leave you to chat, girls. Would you like Amelia to come in now? She has been waiting so patiently."

"Yes, that's fine. I'd love to see her."

Amelia quietly entered the luxury bedroom and timidly came and sat quietly in the bedside chair. Philippa was cross-legged on the bed, next to me, holding my hand.

"What have you been doing to yourself?" Amelia asked. "I've been worried to death about you. Ashley feels terrible, and so does Jon. They are downstairs wondering what on earth is going on."

The concern on her face twisted it into expressions I did not recognise. I felt a pang of guilt as she told me how worried everyone was. I now realised how much my actions had hurt Ashley. But it would hurt him even more if he knew the truth.

"I'm sorry, I can't explain. You wouldn't understand." I said.

"Try me!" Amelia was not going to be fobbed off that easily.

"Well, you know that night Ashley and I came back to your place after Nathan's party?"

"Yes.You were acting very strange. Very quiet?"

"Something happened that I've kept to myself. I haven't even told my mum. Ashley knows a little, but not the whole truth."

"What happened?" Philippa asked, wide-eyed.

Both were now looking at me very anxiously.

"*What* does Ashley know?" they both asked in unison.

"Well, he knows I was attacked. But I never told him to what extent. We came round to your house after the party, and I withheld what had actually happened to me. I told Ashley that Nathan and I had been arguing about his drug taking. I said he'd pushed me and I fell and hit my head and was a bit dizzy. I don't really know how I managed to bottle up my hysteria, but I did, somehow." I looked at both of them and then stared at the floor. "Tonight," I said, my voice a whisper, "that hysteria manifested as attempted suicide."

"You're not making any sense and saying things so matter of factly, Orianna, its not you," Amelia observed. "There must be more to what happened than what you are letting on."

"Okay, well if you want to know what happened, you had better ask Nathan Cooper."

"I can't do that and anyway, I want to ask *you*. I'm your friend and I hope you feel you can trust me and Philippa, enough to know that we would support you."

"Yes, but… it's awful, though. I'm too ashamed to share it. I don't know what you'll think of me?"

"You can tell us, Orianna. Perhaps if you share things, the situation will seem easier?" Philippa said gently.

Tears began to well up in my eyes and once they began to spill down my cheeks they just kept coming. Fighting for control, I started to tell them of my ordeal of Nathan raping me.

Amelia and Philippa sat in shocked silence, horrified to hear the truth.

"You must report this, Orianna—"

"No. And you must not tell anyone. Not a soul. Not even Ashley knows the whole truth. He will hate me and never want to be involved with me again." My voice quivered with emotion. I could not now imagine life without him. How could I go on without my best friend? It didn't bear thinking about.

But Philippa was still pushing for justice. "You must try and speak to my brother, surely he would understand? In fact, I *know* he would. Don't underestimate him – he is an amazing human being. I know he loves you and that he wouldn't abandon you. Shall I ask him to come up and see you? I know he'll be anxious to know that you are okay."

"No, I can't tell him…I really can't. But I don't want to lose him. I just don't know what to do. I'm so confused right now." Tears began rolling down my face again. I felt completely out of control of the whole situation. How could I tell Amelia I was pregnant? I knew that, sooner rather than later, I would have to deal with it. Could I tell them? I had to trust *someone*. Amelia would judge me from her Christian viewpoint. I couldn't tell her…well, not yet.

Philippa gave me a knowing look. Very astute, she knew I had left something unsaid. She half-smiled at me and spoke to Amelia.

"Amelia, why don't you go down and ask my mum if she can get you and Orianna some food? Neither of you have eaten, it will make you both feel better. You have been so kind, coming and staying with Orianna."

"You're sure your mum won't mind?"

"Of course not. She wants to help and thinks a lot of you and Orianna."

With that, Amelia left the room.

❧ Twelve ❧

"Now," Philippa said, moving closer, "are you going to tell me what is *really* going on? I know there's something else. I can see it in your eyes."

My eyes always gave me away when I lied. *Especially* when I lied.

"Ashley is more than besotted by you. I know he's only 17 and you think he can't possibly feel as he does. I know him. I have never seen him like this over anyone – so I know what he feels is real. I'm sure he would stay with you no matter what," Philippa insisted.

"He won't! I know it." Blubbering through my tears, feeling fear, I didn't know what to say or how to say it.

"Just talk to me, Orianna. I will listen and try to understand."

I looked her straight in the eye. "I'm pregnant!" There, it was out in the open. I lowered my eyes in shame, and played with the lace on the bed covers.

"What? Oh, Orianna, I am so sorry. Now I see why you have wanted to keep it to yourself, why you tried to…do what you did." She enfolded me in her arms, hugging me sympathetically.

I had to admit, it did feel better to share the problem, but of course the tears gushed again. This time they just would not stop.

Suddenly, a quiet voice was heard from behind the bedroom door.

"Philippa, could you open the door?" Amelia's voice broke the endearing embrace. She entered the room, carrying a tray filled with toasted sandwiches, tea and biscuits. Amelia set it down on the dressing table, shocked that I was sobbing again.

"Whatever's the matter now?"

Philippa flashed me a quick, but knowing look.

"It's up to you to share it, Orianna. We are both here to support you, no matter what happens, or what you decide."

Amelia sat on the end of the bed. "Are you going to let me in on this? I want to help."

"Before you both jump to conclusions, it's not Ashley's."

"What's not Ashley's?" Amelia asked.

"The baby, or should I say … *foetus*?"

"You're pregnant?" Amelia gasped, her expression frozen in horror.

I knew telling her would be a bad idea. "Yes, and it's Nathan's."

"Oh, my..!" Amelia still looked shocked.

"You and Philippa are the only ones to know. I haven't told anyone else. I just didn't know how to."

"How long have you known?" Philippa asked.

"Six weeks or so."

"And you have told no one else?" Amelia had switched to her *I'm in control*, Gestapo, mode.

"I've just said, so, Amelia. No!" I didn't want all this questioning. I just wanted everything to go back to how it was before Nathan did what he did.

"How on earth have you coped?"

"I haven't. That's why I did what I did tonight. I don't want a baby, especially not *this* baby!"

"Will you get an abortion, then?" Philippa asked.

"I have no other option – I can't keep a baby that was conceived during rape."

"Well," Amelia said, trying to reason with me, "there's also adoption and keeping … it."

"Don't even ask such a thing of me!" I was furious and spat the words at her. What, I wondered would she do, in my shoes?

"Look, now is not the time to discuss this. We should let the dust settle – see how things look tomorrow. Orianna has been through so much already. Let's eat, and discuss this some other time." Philippa's reasoning was directed at Amelia.

Silence fell on the room and each of us was lost in our own thoughts as we started on the sandwiches and tea. The grand, spacious bedroom suddenly seemed tiny; too small for the multitude of thoughts that swirled around the room from each of us. I wanted to change the subject completely. I hated bad or strained atmospheres.

"So do you think our mums will realise our double bluff?" I asked. "You saying you are staying at my place and me saying I am staying at yours when we both know that's not the case?"

"Well, we are both staying together, so it's no big deal, is it? In any case, Mum never checks, she trusts me. I know we shouldn't lie, but in the circumstances, with your near-death experience, we had no choice." Amelia could sometimes be very blunt.

"Philippa, do you know how Ashley came to find me in the car in the first place?"

"I'm not entirely sure. He knew you'd been unhappy about Nathan and the party and said you'd been preoccupied for weeks – different, he said. He was very worried about you. Apparently, Jon saw you driving down a country road and thought you were coming to see Ashley. When you didn't show, Ashley tried to reach you on your mobile phone, but it wouldn't connect. He was worried, and he and Jon decided to see if they could find you. He phoned Amelia and Jack, but no one knew where you were. They drove around some of your favourite haunts until they found you."

"Just in the nick of time!" Amelia chimed in.

"He really loves me, doesn't he?"

"I've told you so!" Philippa confirmed.

"I'm realising that now. I just go around with this big cloud over my head about how I am perceived. And I'm not being obsessive, just realistic."

"What do you mean?"

"Well, I guess because of how I walk and what I look like, I tend to think that no one likes me, let alone that someone like Ashley would fancy me. I never expected him to fall in love with me."

"Jack fancies you," Amelia said, hoping I wouldn't confirm it.

"No, he doesn't! He just flirts – you know what he is like."

"Hmm, I think differently. I see the way he looks at you!"

"Don't be silly, Amelia, you are just imagining it."

"Looks guys, I think it's best we all get some sleep now, it's after midnight!" Philippa could see how tired I was, drained even. "I'll be just down the hallway if you need me. I hope you sleep well," Philippa said, giving me a goodnight hug.

"Okay, we'll speak in the morning. Things will seem clearer then." Amelia also hugged me and left. She closed the door and all was silent.

Once the girls had left, I lay there in the darkness of the bedroom. I had not given much thought to Ashley whilst I had been talking to the girls. Now I was beginning to feel guilty and rather sad, because I sensed somehow that once Ashley knew I'd been raped and was pregnant, our relationship would be over. Fate had deemed it impossible for us to remain together – I knew that now. Again the tears began to flow as I thought of Ashley and the consequences of Nathan's actions.

My mind was all over the place and I felt tired from trying to work out solutions to a problem that may never be resolved. I wondered what Ashley was thinking and what he actually thought of me. Life was definitely hard. I told myself that death would have been easier, even if it was "the coward's way out". God would be sitting with his head in his hands in despair, watching all this unfold.

I was not as religious as Amelia. I believed in God; he just didn't seem personal to me. Why on earth would he care about me? My low self-esteem was in evidence again.

Amelia said she prayed about *everything*. Maybe that was the answer to *everything*. God was omnipotent, right? Was I copping out by asking God to take responsibility for my life? After all, God must know me inside out, whether I believed in him or not? He'd given me free will and the right to choose for myself. Sometimes, I just didn't want that responsibility. Just this once, I would have liked him to take away the burdens I carried.

I was emotionally, physically and mentally drained. What was I holding on for? I had no idea what my future would hold, or even if I had much of a future left. Life without Ashley would be impossible. I was certain about three things: firstly, Ashley didn't know I had been raped or was pregnant; secondly, although he loved me, there was no doubt he would reject me – and he would fight Nathan; thirdly, I was, unfortunately for him, irrevocably and unconditionally in love with him.

I turned on my side and tried to sleep; I had to stop analysing – I felt like my head was going to explode!

The following morning was the same as the night before, with everyone fussing around me. Rose came in first, and with her, the familiar aroma of toast and cereals. She plumped up the pillows until I was propped up in bed by clouds of soft feather and down at my back and shoulders. The teacup clunked as she set the tray down on my lap.

"How are you feeling this morning, dear?" As usual, she looked as if she had just stepped off the cover of *Vogue*, with not a hair out of place. Despite her immaculate appearance, she was kind, considerate, and caring. It was clear that she was devoted to her own family. Yes, she had a busy social life apart from her fund-raising work, but she always had time for her children and friends.

"Did you manage to sleep okay?" she asked.

"Yes, thank you, Mrs Mason." I smiled at her, hoping that it would express my gratitude for all her family's kind support, despite my irresponsible actions. No doubt there would be a further inquisition today. Amelia would want answers. Was I prepared to give them? I felt like a criminal, convicted without trial. I was still confused, not knowing the best solution to my problems. When Rose had entered the room, she had broken my train of thought.

"Would you like me to send the girls in? Stephen would also like to check how you are later on. Is that okay?"

How could I refuse their kind help? At least my being there had relieved me of having to deal with Mum. She would have thrown a fit had she known what was going on.

"Is there anything else I can get you?"

"No, thank you, Mrs Mason. I will be fine, thanks," I lied.

"Call me *Rose*, Orianna. Let's have nothing formal, please," she smiled. "When you are ready, feel free to come down and join everyone."

Ten minutes later, Amelia and Philippa joined me. Philippa came dancing into the bedroom, like a woman without a care in the world.

"Morning!" they both sang in unison. Amelia crept around the door, a little more reserved than normal.

"How are you this morning?" she asked.

"Did you sleep well?" from Philippa.

"Great, thank you." I was lying again. "I've made some decisions, so I know things can go either way.

"What do you mean?" Amelia looked puzzled, wondering what I had come up with.

"Well, I am definitely not getting a termination. And I am definitely not keeping it."

"Adoption, then?" Amelia looked pleased with herself, as if she had pushed me in the right direction.

"Definitely not that, either."

"You're not going to keep the baby, are you?" They both looked shocked, not really understanding what I was suggesting.

"Amelia, you are always going on about a God who cares for you, and each and every person on this planet, right? Well, why can't he deal with this, in the way he sees fit? He is supposed to know me better than anyone, so who better to sort everything out?"

"That's putting God to the test!" Amelia exclaimed, shocked.

"No, it's not. God is the *only* one who can deal with this situation in a responsible way that would suit everyone. Doesn't he know best?"

"Well, I suppose so," Amelia replied sheepishly, knowing I was right, of course.

"I'm not a religious person, as you know, but I respect what you are saying. What do you intend to do?" Philippa asked.

"Pray. Prayers and more prayers. I need you to back me up in this, Amelia. I have never asked anything of God, apart from new legs, when I was a little girl. I can't live with the fact that the father of my child is a rapist and the child was conceived during rape. I couldn't have a baby at my age anyway – especially not with my physical complications," I kept my eyes on the toast I was buttering.

"I understand, but I still think you are testing God!"

I knew Amelia wanted to argue, but she had no choice but to go along with what I wanted.

Philippa wanted a solution that would suit me best. Being older, she didn't believe in arguments and disagreements. She sat on the bed, anxiously twiddling her hair. I was hoping Amelia wasn't going to accelerate the conversation into an argument.

Philippa sympathetically smiled in my direction. "Let's do this, then, and see what God wants. I suggest we sit together and ask God to deal with this right now, as if he were here in this room."

"He is," Amelia said quietly.

A hush fell over the room. The atmosphere changed completely, as Amelia started praying "in tongues". Apart from her hushed voice, the room was just so quiet and still. There was a certain heaviness in the air, but nothing oppressive; just peaceful and calm. As Amelia asked God and the Holy Spirit to come into the room, we began to smell the fresh spring fragrance of apple blossom, a sweet, yet delicate fragrance. Was this an indication of God's presence? The hair on the back of my neck stood up, as I absorbed the atmosphere through every fibre of my being. Slowly, and gently, it enveloped me in pure love.

None of us could utter a word. It was wondrous and awesome – even Philippa felt His presence. She squeezed my hand in acknowledgement and I squeezed hers back, to show her I knew what she meant. Amelia was fidgeting nervously with the buttons on her cardigan and didn't seem sure what else to do. So I prayed.

"God, you know me better than anyone else. You were there at the start, knitting me together in my mother's womb. You know better than anyone what I can cope with and you know I'm pregnant and how this came about. I can't have this baby, especially when Nathan raped me. I know there is a potential life growing inside me, but having this baby would never work."

Tears rolled down my sad and sorry face. I felt overwhelmed with emotion; angry, upset and frustrated all at the same time.

"I don't want to test you," I continued, closing my eyes as tightly as I could. "Please let me miscarry this baby. Take the responsibility from me. Please help me get my life back on track.

I never asked for this and surely I don't deserve it? Lord, I'm begging for your help."

Amelia continued, praying out loud for the same thing, for me. Now I knew she understood. After Amelia had finished talking to the man "upstairs" we felt we had jointly done all we could do, in that moment; finally, a group hug seemed to seal the secret.

"I know it's going to be all right," Philippa said.

"Orianna, I just want to say this," Amelia paused for a second, trying to smile. "Jesus loves you for who you are. He can overcome this mess, I promise. Have faith. Remember when you first gave your life to Jesus, when we were little? He even knows your thoughts before you think them. Trust him, it will be O.K." She quoted some verses of scripture, looking them up on her iPhone bible app. Scrolling through them, she read them aloud to me as if quoting them into the air would somehow permeate my situation and make everything better.

Activity was carrying on as normal downstairs, as if no dramas had occurred here the night before. The TV was blasting out from the games room, as Philippa's younger brother played his console. Voices drifted up from the kitchen, and the phone rang insistently.

"Right," I decided, "I'm going to get showered and dressed. I need to get back to "normal" as soon as possible. Mum will freak out if I don't get home today."

Amelia and Philippa were already dressed. They waited for me, sitting on the bed, chatting. As I emerged, showered, dressed and presentable, the house seemed strangely quiet; all we could hear now were hushed voices from downstairs.

"Do you mind if I go and see if everything is okay?" Philippa seemed tense as she left the room.

"I wonder what's going on." Amelia looked through the bedroom window as we heard the sound of car tyres spinning on the gravel drive below.

"Who was that?"

"Ashley and Jon, I think."

"Oh no!" I shouted. "Do you think Philippa has spilt the beans?"

"She wouldn't...I'm positive."

"Why on earth would he speed off like that?"

"Perhaps we should go down and see what's going on?"

"Good idea." I hoped we weren't walking into family arguments which were not our business.

As we entered the kitchen, the talking stopped and everyone looked up, staring in my direction.

The Masons smiled at me, awkwardly, hardly able to look me in the eye. What was wrong now?

"Sit down, dear. Stephen and I need to talk with you."

It sounded serious and I obliged them. Amelia handed my breakfast tray to Rose and she loaded the dishwasher, busying herself as we talked.

"I have just had a call from Gary," Stephen said. "He got your test results back."

What little colour I had drained instantly from my face.

"Everything has come back fine," Stephen assured me, "apart from one thing, that is."

"What's that?" I knew instinctively what he was going to say and braced myself.

"You are pregnant. The urine tests confirmed it."

"I understand from Ashley that the baby is not his. Is that right?" Stephen's voice was firm, yet remarkably calm.

"You told Ashley?" My head was spinning again, I felt as if I was going to faint.

"Rose, give Orianna a glass of water, please."

I sipped the cold water as Stephen continued. "He overheard. I'm sorry. There was nothing we could do about it. He's gone out with Jon in the car...he said, to clear his head. He'll be okay—"

Philippa broke in. "I couldn't tell him anything, not without your agreement. He will calm down. You can talk to him when he gets back."

"Now I feel so bad. He's going to hate me, for sure!"

Philippa stood beside me, putting her arm around my shoulders.

"Don't worry. I told you before, Ashley is very level-headed. You underestimate what he feels for you. Give him time to think things through. He'll be fine."

"Erm, what's happened here, exactly? Whose baby is it?" Stephen was insistent, knowing that something was very wrong.

I reddened. Tears, never very far away, welled up in my eyes again, remembering that bastard, Nathan. I took a deep breath, snuffling loudly.

"It's Nathan Cooper's. He raped me."

Rose stopped her pottering and gasped.

"Oh, Orianna, no! I'm so sorry." Deep concern shone out from her familiar blue eyes, reminding me so much of Ashley.

Stephen immediately offered his support. "Now we understand the reasons behind your actions last night, and we will protect you. Help you. That's why we got Gary to come and see you last night; we didn't want to call the police because of how you were found. Although, under the circumstances, it would be a good idea for you to get some counselling through your GP's surgery. You also need to get some support from your family now too. It's very important that you do." His tone was grave and serious.

"Ashley also made a choice to have you as his girlfriend and as such we have to support him in that, as you are with Ashley now, and a part of this family."

His words reassured me, but still didn't make my predicament with the pregnancy and Ashley seem any easier.

"Perhaps it would be best if I wasn't in Ashley's life?" My stomach was churning, reacting to the utter turmoil in my head.

135

"Don't say things like that! Does Nathan know, by the way?"

"No, not yet."

"What do you want to do about it?"

"I just want it all to go away."

Stephen shook his head. "It won't, will it? Not with a baby growing inside you. I'm so sorry to be blunt, but we have to face facts. Now, have you thought about what you want to do? We will support you whatever you decide."

Amelia and Philippa exchanged knowing glances. Did they think I was mental, asking God to deal with this situation? In the circumstances, it seemed the only *right* and sensible thing to do. When would my brain stop aching with these issues? I was worried about Ashley. How was he? What was he thinking? What did he think of me? He must be so confused right now, driving off like that. But at least he had Jon with him. He was a sensible guy, straight forward and calm. He would know what to say to Ashley.

Stephen's voice broke the silence.

"Would you like me to go with you to see Nathan and his dad? Don't you think Nathan should be aware of what's happening?"

"Definitely not!" I began to panic. "Please, just let me deal with this in my own way, and in my own time ... "

"Okay, okay. I respect your wishes. I'm not going to push you."

I really appreciated their efforts to help, but pressurising me was not the answer.

"I will speak to Nathan when I am ready. Please ... let me handle it myself."

Philippa threw me a worried look. Did she think I couldn't deal with this? Everyone seemed to be treating me with kid gloves. I was much more concerned with how Mum would deal with things, if she found out. She would worry herself to death, blow things up out of all proportion. I was going to wait and see if my prayers were going to be answered. Surely God would come through for me. How on earth would I get through this otherwise? A disabled, pregnant teenager – that would really be great on my CV – not!

What a situation to be in; it felt as if I was being wrapped in concrete and allowed to set.

"You have all been so wonderful," I told them, "but I really can't impose on you like this."

"We want to help, that's all," Rose said. "You are not imposing on us. But perhaps you need some outside support, like the rape crisis line, or something. They can give the kind of counselling that we would find impossible to give."

Stephen still thought that Nathan should be made aware of his responsibilities. "Have you thought about reporting Nathan?"

"Nathan is over 16, I'm over 16. It's my word against his. I don't want to get into a situation like that."

"It's your decision, as I said before," Stephen said, "but he should be made accountable and punished – *something* needs to be done."

I'd had enough. Tears were threatening again and I struggled for control. "I promise, Mr Mason, that I will deal with him in my own way."

Amelia's intervention was timely and I could have kissed her. "Orianna, don't you think we should go back to Wimborne? Get you sorted out and go and see your mum?"

"Yes, that *is* a good idea." I looked over at Philippa. "Can you let Ashley know that I will talk to him as soon as he's ready?"

"I will. He'll be back later, I'm sure. Perhaps you'll be able to meet up?"

Our departure was emotional. Mrs Mason gave me a huge hug, as did Philippa, and Stephen gave me a peck on the cheek, which had me blushing, for some reason. He was a bit of a charmer, just like his sons!

"Remember, if you need anything, just ask." I smiled back, knowing that he really meant it, and his attitude to Nathan was all part of his desire to help.

"Come on, Orianna, we need to get going."

We got into our respective cars, the extra apendages on my car from the night before were gone. There was no trace of what had happened, leaving the Masons on their doorstep, Stephen and Rose holding hands, still in love after all these years. As they waved us off, I wondered what they would be saying about me in private. But my biggest worry was Ashley. I knew he wouldn't want to go on seeing me now, even if God did answer my prayers.

❧ Thirteen ❦

In order to avoid a confrontation with Mum, Amelia and I hatched a plan to cover our tracks. There was no way I was going to let her know I was pregnant, not if I could help it. So we just went along with the story that I had stayed at Amelia's, and that was it. She bought it, which I knew she would. I hated lying to her, but I wanted to save her the pain of my current situation.

Mum was in the lounge, painting her toenails. Of course, there would be a barrage of questions, but I was prepared for that.

"So, how have you both been, then?" Mum asked, looking up from her screaming red toenails.

"Great, thanks." Amelia threw me a quick glance.

"Did you forget your stuff?"

Uh-oh; here we go.

"Yes, it was a last minute decision. We started talking, and forgot about the time last night. It just flew…sorry. I hope you weren't worried?"

"No, I know you are both sensible girls and I knew where you were, so it wasn't a problem."

I winced inside as I realised how much she trusted me and how devastated she would be if she knew the truth.

I had felt slightly queasy all morning, but a sudden wave of nausea swept over me. Now was the time to hit the loo.

"Excuse me a minute; I need the bathroom." I moved as quickly as I could, trying not to look desperate. Hell! Morning sickness wasn't going to be easy to hide…

After the sickness had subsided and the flush of the toilet had eliminated the evidence, I returned to the lounge. I could hear Mum interrogating Amelia.

"Has Orianna got a boyfriend yet?"

"It's not really for me to say, Mrs Stewart," I heard Amelia reply in her usual shy way when she felt confronted and hated telling white lies.

"That must mean she has, then! I wondered why she seemed so much happier lately. I don't like to pry, but I had hoped she might tell me herself."

"He's nice, really and truly. You couldn't have wanted a nicer boyfriend for her. He is so thoughtful, caring, sensib—" she stopped mid sentence, as I entered the kitchen.

Mum was walking around on her heels on the tiles, with kitchen roll wrapped in between each toe, so the polish wouldn't get smudged. Typical Mum.

Amelia blushed, obviously realising she had probably said far too much.

"Oh, hey, Amelia, what are you talking about, then? I tried to appear as if I had not overheard them.

"We had so much fun, didn't we? A really lazy sleepover, hey?" She was a terrible liar. She launched into a minute-by-minute account of the previous night, hoping it would convince Mum we really *did* have a sleepover.

Strangely hungry now, after the emergency dash to the loo, I made some toast. When her polish was dry, Mum put the kettle on.

"What are you going to do with the rest of your day, then?"

"I'm going to head off home, Mrs Stewart."

"And you, Orianna. What about you?"

"This afternoon I think I'll hang out here, if that's okay with you?"

"Where were you *really*… last night and this morning?"

I should have known I wouldn't get away with it that easily. I couldn't lie completely.

"I was over at the Masons."

She dropped her teaspoon on the floor. "The Masons? I've heard of them. Isn't there a surgeon at the private hospital called Mr Mason? What were you doing up there?"

"Well, I had a date with Ashley Mason, and he wanted to introduce me to his parents."

Mum appeared as if she was about to have some kind of attack.

"Mum, are you all right?"

"You are going out with that Mason boy?" she screeched. "From what I have heard about him, he's too old for you, isn't he?"

"I thought you wanted me to have a boyfriend?"

"I'm not sure *he's* right for you."

"We're both in sixth form, Mum. He's a sixth former, I'm a sixth former, right?"

"Aren't they a large family? Hang on … which one is Aston?"

"It's *Ashley* and he's not the oldest or the youngest. He's the middle one with the dark hair and blue eyes. The beautiful one, the god-like one … "

"Oh. Well, that's better … I guess."

"What do you mean?"

"At least he is your age. His family are well to do, aren't they?" She annoyed me with the fact that she was pleased he came from a monied family.

"Mum, money doesn't matter. It's who they are that counts!"

"So, is he your boyfriend?" Mum looked puzzled, as if she didn't really want to know the answer to that question.

"Sort of, I guess." I looked at her through my lashes, hoping to avoid getting a lecture.

"You told me you weren't interested in having a boyfriend." She picked up the teaspoon again, so the worst was over.

"Well, Ashley came along and I changed my mind. Okay?"

She gave me a disparaging look as she sipped her tea. Amelia chewed on a slice of toast, not wanting to miss the outcome of the conversation.

"So when are you going to introduce me?" Mum looked at me sternly, as if she wanted things resolved right now.

"Not yet. But I will, I promise. It's early days, Mum," I pleaded.

"You'd better introduce me, young lady, otherwise he won't be allowed in the house," she declared, folding her arms in annoyance.

"Oh, come on, Mum! Don't be so old fashioned!"

Since when did she become all Victorian on me? It was okay for her to be a floozie with all her blind dates, but not for me to actually have a boyfriend. Sometimes she could be such a hypocrite.

"I'm not. I need to know the boy my daughter is dating is right for her!" She was almost shouting now. This was getting just a little bit intense – and I thought I had a laid-back mum. She stood there with her arms still folded and nostrils flaring. She looked really angry. I had hoped she'd be happy for me, after all, she'd been begging me to get a boyfriend for months, and now I had one she didn't seem to like it. I'd never understand parents. Ever.

I tried to change tactics, hoping she'd see sense.

"All you need to know is that Ashley is amazing. If he hadn't have come along, I'm sure I'd end up with just *anyone*. I never thought someone decent and worthwhile like Ashley would want me … being disabled and everything. I reckoned that by the time I hit 40, I'd end up like you – divorced with two kids to look after

– and who would want me then, eh?" Maybe I'd gone too far, but I was seething inside and talking back to her somehow seemed appealing.

"Don't talk so silly, Orianna." Mum's face had begun to soften.

"I'm not being silly, just realistic," I said, like a petulant child, whose mum never listened to her.

"That's your answer to everything, my girl!" Her anger flared again briefly. There was so much tension in the room, I almost laughed, because it was ridiculous.

"Honestly, Mum, he is right for me. I promise you I wouldn't be with him otherwise." I hoped that convinced her that I could be mature.

Amelia sat at the kitchen table observing Mum and twisting her low-lights between her fingers.

"I'll leave you to sort it out," Mum huffed. "I'm off down the market, see you later."

I could smell her perfume as she brushed past me, grabbing her coat and handbag. She slammed the door behind her.

"Well, that was awkward!" Amelia grimaced. "I didn't think your mum got stressed like that?"

I frowned. "She can do. Especially when she doesn't agree with me or get her own way."

There was a pause, as Amelia and I just looked at each other, not really knowing what else to say.

"Will you stay a while?" I finally asked.

"I haven't finished my toast yet," Amelia mumbled, through a mouthful of crunchy farmhouse. "There's no question that I would stay, you muppet. Of course I will."

I was still very confused about my predicament. "What do you think I should do now?"

"Wait, I suppose. Unless you have changed your mind and want to go through the adoption process?"

Amelia twitched. I could see she didn't want an argument. She stretched her arms out to hug me and I felt so relieved that she was there, being supportive. We clung to each other tightly for several seconds.

"I released myself from her embrace, swaying slightly. I felt a bit light-headed. "It has got to be okay. Can you imagine what my mother would be like if she knew I was pregnant? It just doesn't bear thinking of. You saw what she was like earlier – she'd go ballistic!" I laughed, but this was not a laughing matter. "Why don't we just relax for a while – listen to some music?"

We sat in silence for a few minutes, while Amelia browsed the CD collection trying to choose something to play.

"You know I care about you don't you?"

"Yes, of course," I replied.

"If Ashley won't see you anymore after this, I am always here for you, you know that?"

"What makes you think Ashley won't stay with me?"

I was worried now; she had me thinking the worst. What if he didn't want me anymore? What if I was an embarrassment to him? What would I do without him? I stared out of the window in a daydream, mulling over my thoughts, preoccupied with the future, or lack of it. Amelia broke into my thoughts.

"I know what would be even better – how about we give each other a makeover?" Amelia looked hopeful.

"No, I'm not really in the mood for that. I ought to get on with some school work," I insisted. I just wanted to sit quietly.

Amelia frowned at me. "Are you okay? You don't seem right."

"I do fee…feel a bit dizzy," I stammered, wobbling up onto my feet. The room began to spin around and my ankles gave way beneath me, as I clung to the sofa for stability.

"Look, go and lie down," Amelia said, trying to support me. "You need to relax. You've had a really stressful few weeks." She looked worried and out of her depth.

"Okay. Perhaps you're right," I said through gritted teeth. The room was still spinning.

"I'll bring you a fresh cup of tea," Amelia suggested, trying to think of something useful to do.

Clinging to the banister, I managed to get to the top of the stairs. Suddenly, an excruciating pain ripped through my abdomen. I yelled out in agony, and Amelia hurried to me, spilling the half-made mug of tea along the way. The pain continued to course through my body. I felt hot and sick as I clutched my stomach with both hands, writhing in panic. I almost blacked out, and then gradually, I felt a warm wetness between my thighs.

"Oh, no! The …. pain! Amelia, what's happening?" I was half-screaming, half-shouting. I could feel a steady trickle of warm, thick wetness between my thighs.

"You're bleeding! Honey, you must be having a miscarriage!" The stain flushed through my clothes as Amelia flustered round me, not knowing what quite what to do. If it was seeping through my trousers; I realised I must have been bleeding badly. Chasing downstairs, she found my mobile.

"Is Philippa's number in your phone? I'm going to ring her, okay?"

"It should be," I screamed. I needed an adult here; someone who could take proper charge of what was happening.

I watched her as she found the number and waited for an answer. She was rapidly tapping her thigh, as if urging Philippa to answer her phone. She looked distraught.

"She's not answering!" Amelia was yelling now. "What do you want me to do?"

"I'll just ride it out. I'm only six weeks or so, it won't be much," I groaned.

"How do you know that? You can't do this alone! You need a doctor. Let me get you some painkillers, then," she said, desperate to do something to make me feel better. Her words tumbled in a flurry as she panicked. I wished she'd shut up and just let me get on with it. It would have been nice if Mum was here for support, but I knew it would be the wrong thing to phone her.

"Thanks." Not that Paracetamol would help much. I could feel the pain ripping through my stomach again. My vision was blurred from the tears that were welling up. I had never felt this low before. I could hear Amelia speaking as calmly as she could on my mobile.

"Yes, it's Miss Stewart. She needs a house visit, as soon as possible!"

There was a pause.

"Her symptoms? It's simple; she's bleeding down below, has chronic stomach cramps and is approximately six weeks pregnant."

Another pause.

"Yes, that's what I said," Amelia said insistently. "What? No house visit? But she needs a doctor!"

There was another long pause. Amelia looked angry.

"Thanks for nothing!" I heard her yell as she finished the call.

"Wha...what's the matter?" I panted through the pain.

"They said you don't need a house call. Your body will do what it needs to do, and then you go and get a check up when it's all over."

Neither of us could believe that a helpline could be so *un*helpful.

I staggered into the bathroom where Amelia left me to clean myself up and change. I sat on the toilet seat, unsure of getting out of my now heavily soiled clothes. After a while I heard her knocking at the door.

"Are you okay in there?" Amelia sounded helpless.

"Yes, I'll be out in a minute."

I decided I had better change. Dumping the soiled clothes in a pile, the water heater jerked into action as the overhead shower began to cover me in hot water. I stood there, closing my eyes, trying to avoid looking at the steady stream of red that had joined the run of clear water down the plughole. Eventually, I put on my nice clean dressing gown. The shower had refreshed me and I was relieved that the pain was starting to subside. I crept into the hallway, clutching my bloodstained knickers and jeans. I felt both elated and sad at the same time. I had got what I prayed for – an end to my hated pregnancy. I hadn't bargained for the pain and trauma; it had only been a tiny embryo…hadn't it?

"I'm going to put this lot in the washing machine – hide the evidence."

"Here." Amelia held out her arms. "Let me take it."

I handed the washing to her.

"Shall I make you a fresh cuppa?" she asked.

"Tea? A soddin' brandy would be more like it! I didn't realise the pain would be that bad, but at least it'll soon be over with now. Well, almost."

"What do you mean, *almost*?" Amelia's face was screwed up.

"Well, I still have to deal with Nathan, and then there's Ashley."

"Um, oh yeah."

"And my mother!" I exclaimed, almost frozen at the thought.

"She'll need to know, eventually," Amelia nodded.

"Maybe, but not just yet, eh?" I pleaded quietly.

Tentatively, I went downstairs, a step at a time, trying to avoid making the throbbing pain in my belly any worse. Amelia followed, still clutching the laundry. The kitchen floor struck icily cold to my bare feet as I plodded across the tiles. It really did seem like a miracle that I'd miscarried so quickly. Would God really come through for me that quickly? I felt dazed, exhausted, relieved and confused as I shoved the washing from the kitchen worktop into the machine.

'Ping' went the dial on the washer-dryer, as I set it to 60 degrees. That would destroy the evidence!

"I told you things would get better!" Amelia exclaimed, in a fake elated way. I knew she was trying to make me feel better, but her hugs of sympathy were making me feel nauseous; not with her, but with the whole situation.

"What will you say to your mum?" she enquired.

"I don't know. I'll just tell her I've got a stomach bug, or something – having had to rush to the bathroom this morning will at least make a virus seem more genuine."

We both jumped as my mobile phone rang.

It was Jack. "Hi, babes, how's you?"

"I can't talk right now, I'm not feeling well, but Amelia can fill you in. I'll pass the phone to her." I was in no mood to socialise.

Amelia made up a feeble excuse, but it didn't dissuade Jack. Once he got an idea in his head that was it.

"I have to speak to Orianna – it's really important!" I could hear him bellowing down the phone.

"You can't, she's not well and she needs to rest!"

"Fine. If you won't let me see her, I'm coming round – this is an emergency!"

Amelia cocked her head to one side, listening. "Here he comes," she said, going over to the window. Within five minutes or so, as promised, he turned up.

Pop-pop-pop-pop-pop-pop... it was the unmistakeable sound of Jack's Vespa 50 approaching. I joined Amelia at the window and we watched him dismount. The stupid thing almost toppled over as he parked it because of the weight of the multiple mirrors adorning the front. The squirrel-tail aerial flapped furiously in the stiff breeze. Jack had his collar pulled up against the wind chill, and looked like he had two left feet as he came stumbling up to the front door, nearly falling into the flower beds in his haste. Why was he racing to my door in such a panic?

The door bell chimed repeatedly and there was an impatient *rap-rap-rap* of the door knocker as he waited for me to answer.

"Speak of the devil and the devil shall appear," Jack announced as I swung the door open.

"Where's the fire?" I laughed. I pulled my dressing gown hard around me, looking a bit sheepish. Jack looked me up and down in a confused manner, not knowing quite where to start. I ushered him throught the front door and then shut it tightly behind him.

"I needed to tell you—" he began, as he came bustling into the lounge, fending off Gio, who was giving him her usual welcome.

"It's Ashley! He had a massive punch-up with Nathan Cooper in the square this morning. He wasn't badly hurt – mostly bruises, I think. Nathan came off worse with a broken nose, cuts and bruises and a monster of a black eye. He had to go to hospital!"

I was fully aware of the reasons, but I had to ask. I tried to remain expressionless, giving nothing away.

"Something to do with you ... what's going on?"

"I don't know. Didn't you ask?"

"Well, no. I couldn't. Ashley's elder brother was there trying to keep them apart – he wouldn't let me near Ashley to ask. I just heard your name being shouted a few times. Ashley was really angry." Jack stared me in the face. "Are you dating him? What the hell is going on?"

I tried not to look shocked, coming from him, the swearing never bothered me. Jack was my friend, but the last thing I wanted was him knowing what was going on right now.

He suddenly blushed. "Why are you in your dressing gown?"

"I told you on the phone. I don't feel well – and don't ask, it's girl stuff," I said defiantly.

"Oh, sorry." He looked at the floor. "It's just that I heard a rumour you were pregnant—"

"What?" I tried to sound really shocked. Well, I was shocked. How the hell did he know that? My stomach was still in knots,

149

partly from the pain and partly from the escalation of my situation. Tears were threatening again. I blinked them back; I couldn't let Jack suspect there had been any truth in the rumour.

"Who did you hear that from?" Amelia asked, trying to stay calm for both of us.

"One of Nathan's mates … not Ashley, but someone else. I've got to be honest, I was shocked. I sort of realised there was something going on between you and Ashley, but I hadn't realised it was that serious!" Jack looked troubled.

"It's not! You are just hearing gossip – it's nothing to worry about," I lied through my teeth. "Ashley was probably being taunted about seeing me, you know what Nathan is like. He's such an ignorant son of a bitch – sorry, guys, but he is!"

I tried to sound mature, as I huddled myself up on the sofa, wrapping the dressing gown tightly around me, protecting my modesty. I took a sip of the tea that Amelia handed to me. It was hot and strong, somehow normal and comforting. I wondered if Ashley was okay. What on earth was going on? Was he hurt? If he'd just stayed away from Nathan, then none of this would have happened. But then I never would have realised how utterly and crazy-in-love with him, I was.

Amelia fidgeted in her seat. She was clearly unhappy about the latest developments in this sorry saga. She wasn't good in confrontational situations and just wanted things to always run smoothly. Didn't we all? However, this was my life we were talking about, and nothing ever ran smoothly. From the moment I was born, things were difficult. According to Mum, I "died" several times, due to my prematurity and low birthweight of 1lb 12oz, but God must have wanted me here, because I had survived.

At this point in time, it wasn't good for me to dwell on the past; my life had to move forward. I had to think of the here and now – of Ashley. That is, if we had a future after all that had happened. As I hadn't seen him for a day, there was no way of knowing what he thought about everything.

"So, how are you really?" Jack enquired again. "You look pale."

"Honestly, I'm fine. I'm shocked about Ashley and Nathan, but apart from that I'm okay."

"Orianna, I'm going to go now, as long as you're okay, right?" Amelia maintained eye contact with me, trying to make sure I really was okay with her leaving. Her coat bunched around her arm as she embraced me.

"Ring me if you need *anything*," she insisted.

"Thanks," I whispered as she released me and made for the door.

"Are you sure you're okay?" Jack persisted again.

"Jack! I've told you, I'm fine. Honestly." He was bugging me now.

"So, what is it about Ashley you like, besides the car, of course?" He laughed as he asked, but I knew he was fishing for some serious answers. "As long as you like me almost the same. And you think I'm good looking, sort of. I'm prepared to be annoyingly persistent, you know."

I was aware of his proximity, as he sat down beside me; not that he made me feel uncomfortable at all, I just didn't want to give him false hopes.

"Don't you ever give up?" I asked.

"No. Not with you."

His reply made me cringe. "Trust me, Jack, we're great as best mates, but nothing more. Ashley is special and that's all I'm going to say."

"I do trust you. You really aren't pregnant, though?"

"I said *no*, didn't I?" Snapping at Jack was not the answer. I needed to speak with Ashley, but the likelihood of that was so remote, it wasn't worth thinking about. Being honest, I felt abandoned by him, even though I'd only spoken to him a day or so previously. The pregnancy and my suicide attempt had cleaved a gigantic void between us, and I didn't how to begin to close it up.

"What's so special about Ashley Mason, then?" Jack sneered at me, trying to hide his disappointment at my having a boyfriend who wasn't him.

"You wouldn't get it," I said, still trying to appear indifferent, unsuccessfully, as it turned out.

"I'm not blind, Orianna!" I can see your reaction when I mention his name. "Okay, so you think he's God's gift to you – I get it!" Now it was Jack's turn to snap. He pulled a face. "Sorry, but I just don't want you to get hurt."

"I know, Jack. I know." Taking his hand in mine, I tried to be kind, hoping I was saying the right thing. "You are an amazing friend and we're good together. We couldn't stay away from each other … we've known each other too long."

"I'm going home, Orianna. I came and told you what I saw. I can't hang out with you any more, at least not if you are dating Ashley. I just couldn't bear to watch you get hurt. He'll chew you up and spit you out." There was sadness in his eyes. "I'm not good enough to be your friend any more, or anything else. I'm not what I was before. I don't think I could try to be friends with Ashley – even for your sake – we are just too different."

As his words tumbled out, I could plainly see that he was upset. Jack the lad, always the happy one was close to breaking down. I'd hurt him now, and there was absolutely nothing I could do.

❧ Fourteen ❦

It didn't matter to me if I ditched school. I really wasn't up to going, anyway. I made up some excuse that I had a bug and Mum dropped me off at the doctor's in the morning. My hands were clammy as I went in, alone, to explain to the doctor about the miscarriage. I was lucky that I had an understanding GP. Being under 18, I still felt vulnerable, concerned that she could breach patient confidentiality and phone my mum.

"No, it's against the law for me to tell your mum anything without your consent." Doctor Griffith examined my tummy with her cold, prodding fingers. The internal examination was the worst. A bright light shining into the opening between my legs was not my idea of how to spend a Monday morning, so I just shut my eyes until the doctor had finished and said I could get dressed.

She binned the bloodied examination gloves and washed her hands. "Orianna, you will need another check-up when the bleeding has stopped completely, but as far as I can tell at the moment, you seem fine. Everything seems to have disengaged and fallen away. I think it's over, but I'll book you in for a scan, just to make sure."

A scan? God, I didn't want any more fuss.

"Do I have to?"

She smiled. "Have a scan? There's nothing to it, and it will confirm that everything—"

"I don't want a scan," I told her. "You said everything seemed fine?"

"As far as I can tell, yes, but—"

"That's good enough for me, then."

"Orianna, I can't force you to do something you clearly don't want to do and I suspect that even if I make the appointment, you won't attend. But I want you to take a course of antibiotics to eliminate the chances of an infection, and if you feel at all unwell in the next two weeks or so, you must let me know. Do you understand?"

I nodded. Mum would think the antibiotics were for the "bug" I'd invented.

"Do you need any painkillers?"

"No, thanks. The pain is not too bad now."

"Your hormones will take a while to settle down and you may feel depressed. Would you like me to refer you to a counsellor?"

"Definitely not, thank you. I'm fine." "I'm fine" seemed to be my stock phrase; it covered a multitude of feelings and gave a blanket response to almost any personal question.

"Okay. I have to ask." Dr Griffith handed me a prescription. "Three times a day before food for ten days. Make sure you complete the course."

"Thanks for your time, doctor. I appreciate you examining me today – it's given me peace of mind."

"Glad to help. Is there anything else?"

There wasn't. I kept my head down as I walked out of the surgery and crossed the road to go the pharmacy. Glad to be rid of the physical consequences of the rape, I slowly walked back home. The walk would do me good, even though it hurt. The fresh air would help, at least.

I decided that I was better thinking about the rape and the pregnancy as if it had happened to another person. That way I could detach myself from it and try and get on with my life. I still didn't fancy going into school today – it could wait.

Arriving home, however, I still felt very confused by the events of the last few days. My thoughts were all over the place and it was difficult to separate dreams from nightmares or fantasy from reality. It was going to take me some time to adjust to everything that had happened to me.

I took the stairs up to my room slowly, trying to forget why I wasn't at school. Gio came in with me and I closed the door behind us, shutting out the rest of the world.

I perched on the edge of my rumpled duvet. Should I read a book? I made myself comfortable, lying on the bed with Gio snuggled up beside me. I flicked through my fashion illustration book, taking in the ornate diagrams and reading the tips and ideas. Then I decided something less academic would be more relaxing and searched through my bookcase. I found a hard back copy of *Pride and Prejudice* – that would do. I'd get lost with Mr Darcy for a while…

I woke up with a jolt. The door bell was ringing. What time was it? I had drifted off to sleep. Gio was off the bed, insistently barking at the bedroom door. I looked at my bedside clock. Four-thirty. God! I'd been asleep for hours. Perhaps it was Amelia, back to see if I was all right?

When I was halfway down the stairs, I could see a tall figure silhouetted against the glass panel of the front door. It certainly wasn't Amelia. Perhaps it was Jack, come to pester me again, bless him. As I opened the door, I was surprised to see Ashley standing there in the rain. A Greek god in a navy blue trench coat! He leaned against the porch entrance to close his large umbrella.

"Philippa dropped me off. I didn't see you at school today, so I thought I'd call by."

"Hi, that's very kind. You'd better come in. How long's it been raining?"

"Started as we came out of school." He hung his coat on the hook in the hall, put his umbrella and bag by the coat stand and followed me into the lounge. Gio, unable to contain her excitement, threw herself at him as he sat on the sofa. I knew how she felt.

"Would you like a cuppa?" I asked, heading for the kitchen.

"That would be great," he smiled.

"So what happened to your face?" I had to bring it up; his jaw and eye were covered in bruises.

"I was defending a friend's honour."

"Who would that have been, then?" I asked innocently.

"You, of course," he said, confirming what I already knew.

"It would be more prudent for you not to be my friend, especially with what I have put you and your family through." I cringed at the thought of my actions over the past few days and wanted to melt into the wall and disappear for ever.

Ashley came into the kitchen. Carrying the mugs, he followed me up to my room. My heart pounded in my chest as I realised Ashley wanted to stay. After everything I had put him through, why would he really want to spend time with me? Setting the cups down on my bedside table, he then sat on my bed like a carving of an Adonis, relaxing against my plumped-up pillows. I smiled, trembling with excitement at the thought of us alone together in my room.

The heady scent of his aftershave permeated the room. Still slightly embarrassed, I smiled at him again. His lips twitched deliciously as he smiled back, his sculpture-like pose coming to life. I watched his eyes appraising me. God, I must have looked a mess – ruffled hair, creased dressing gown and no make-up.

He raised one eyebrow. "You look nice."

I grimaced. I was worried. Should I really be alone in my bedroom in only a dressing gown with my boyfriend? If Mum came home right now and saw me like this, I'm not sure she'd be very happy.

"No, you look great – it looks good on you."

"What does?"

"Sorry, I was teasing," he smiled, looking the dressing gown up and down.

As I lay on the bed next to him, staring at the crack in the ceiling, he slowly raised his hand and stroked my face with his finger.

His caress was so distracting I even found it difficult to form a sentence. I looked into his eyes, taking a moment to focus.

"So... why are you really here?" I asked, and this time I wasn't fishing or pretending. I genuinely wanted to know the answer. I was shocked when I heard it.

"I'm tired of trying to stay away from you, Orianna. Believe me, I've tried for the last day. I was going to finish things with you, I was so angry – but, as I say, I just can't stay away."

"You really should try harder. I'm no good for you," I replied. I wanted to impress upon him, without actually saying it, that he'd be made to look a fool by his friends, if he even considered being with me any more.

"Let me be the judge of that," he said very firmly, now stroking my tangled hair.

"Look, I decided long ago my life was a disaster. Why should it turn out any different now?" I played with the cushions on my bed, and then reached to stroke Gio as she snuggled up with us on the bed. We were like a little extended family.

"You've got me now. I think your friends are angry with me for stealing you, too," Ashley grinned.

"Why do you say that?"

"Jack tried to interfere yesterday when I had a... a scuffle with Nathan in the square." His eyes fixed on one point on the wall, as his conversation turned more serious. "I'm just going to do what I want now and let the chips fall where they may, but I bet you things will change for the better." He was confusing me with conversation. I should have his faith in the situation, especially after the answered prayers. I wasn't used to God coming through for me; I'm not sure my faith ever expected him to. My depth of faith and relationship with God needed to change – my attitude needed to change. In fact, my attitude needed to change towards everything – God, my disability, Ashley and my friends; it all needed to change for the better. Ashley jolted me with his arm.

"Have you gone to sleep?"

"No! You seem very sure of yourself – ever the optimist,with everything," I giggled.

"I always say too much when I'm talking to you – that's one of my problems. And I want to make you one of my problems right now." His tone was still serious as he combed my tangled hair with his fingers.

"What? Ashley, I don't understand what you are on about. Honestly, you give me a headache with your highflying ideas and mood swings."

"You've a bit of a temper, don't you?" I quizzed him. "Me – mood swings? Never." He smirked. "I just thought it would be better to stay away for a bit, while we both got our heads sorted."

"Do you need an aspirin?" I laughed, trying to lighten the mood.

"No!" He laughed with me, then started trying to tickle me as I began giggling uncontrollably.

"Your boyfriend seems to think I'm being unpleasant to you. He was debating whether or not to come and break up the fight I had with Nathan yesterday."

"Jack's just a mate, and you know it!"

"Well, tell him I'm not the bad guy – I want to be the superhero, right?"

"Superhero, huh? Right. And how do you propose to do that?" I teased.

"By *proposing* this." In a flash, he slid off my bed in one quick movement and walked round to my side. I could only watch in utter amazement as he dropped down on one knee, pulled an ivory box from his pocket, and opened it, right under my nose.

"Will you marry me?"

"What?" I gasped. "Are you mad? Why? I can't believe you're asking me this!"

"Why not? You've ditched class for a reason, haven't you? It's healthy to ditch class now and then, even if it is because you feel unwell."

"What? Now you've lost me … "

"Well, I'm asking you to marry me for a reason, too … "

"What reason could there be?" I asked, putting on an act of innocence.

"Wow, you're pink, Orianna! That's the first time I've seen you really blush … " He was enjoying this.

"What's the reason?" I persisted, though I knew my cheeks were now crimson.

"You know why, don't you? I love you and can't live without you," he breathed.

I needed some distraction. I looked at him, helplessly, wishing my blushing would subside.

"So why do you think Nathan and I had a fight?" he quizzed me.

"Cos you finally realised what a prize idiot he is?" I laughed, but I knew I should be trying to be serious at this point.

"Sometimes I have a problem with my temper, Anna. Especially where you are concerned."

"Your temper?" I parroted. "What have I done?"

"Besides trying to gas yourself? Nothing."

"So, elaborate, please."

"Listen to me, Anna," he said in a low voice. "I'm sorry for embarrassing you by fighting over you with Nathan, but I'm not sorry I put him in hospital. I couldn't restrain myself when I ran into him yesterday. Especially when I knew the truth... about the baby."

Now I was cringing inside, which I hoped didn't show. So, he knew the truth. Now I desperately wanted to change the subject.

"That ring dazzles me! How big is that diamond anyway? It's more like a rock!" I laughed, embarrassed that his extravagance was aimed at me.

"Do I dazzle you as well, or is it just the ring?" The corners of his mouth turned up in amusement. "Why not try to be more creative in your avoidance of my main question?" he said. "A straight yes or no will suffice."

"It will cause major headlines in the local press if I say yes." I was serious this time.

"Then just say it... *say* it," he begged.

"Only... you could get into trouble in a town this small. You will devastate all the women in Wimborne by marrying me. They'll be broken-hearted for the next decade, you know."

"Stop teasing me, and let's be serious," Ashley demanded, stroking my face.

"I *am* being serious." My inexperience in these matters was painfully obvious. I didn't know what to say.

"And Nathan's baby? Are you serious about that? Because if you are, I will fully support you, you know," he added.

"No. Don't worry, that's over. I've told you, I'm a magnet for bad luck or good luck, depending on how you view the situation," I replied.

"No. You're not a magnet for bad luck, but you are a magnet for trouble, trouble you don't cause. Nathan is trouble. That's why I beat the hell out of him, I just couldn't stand his attitude any more. When I found out he raped you, I just snapped." Ashley said, with raw anger in his voice. I was amazed at how calm he now was. I guessed that a good night's sleep and thinking on things had obviously done him some good. Violence wasn't the way to solve anything.

"I guess you'd found out the other day, at your place?" I wanted him to confirm that.

"That's right. I overheard Dad talking to Gary on the phone and jumped to the right conclusion. I'm sorry for driving off like that with Jon, but I just couldn't face you. I felt like I had let you down. I wasn't there to protect you – when it happened, I mean – and I should have been. If there is anything dangerous within a ten-mile radius, it will invariably find you." He said it like it was the biggest crime ever committed, and my heart melted.

"Do you really want to be involved with trouble?" I whispered, staring intently into his eyes.

"Ordinary people seem to make it through the day without so many catastrophes. But then, I forgot, you're not ordinary."

"Never have been!" I laughed.

"I'm afraid your number was up the first time I met you."

"Why's that?"

"Not because you tripped in a pothole or anything – but because I knew I was going to fall in love with you!" He grinned at me.

"Oh, right. You knew that?"

"Of course. You know when you know, right?" he chimed.

"It's torn me apart, being away from you." That was my round about way of saying "I love you, too", in response. For some reason, I couldn't get the words out.

"It was very … hard – you can't imagine how hard – for me to simply stay away from you. I have felt so guilty because I should have been there to protect you, to stop all this from happening to you." He was serious, watching my expression.

"It's over now," I said decidedly.

He appeared not to have understood. "Have you told your mum about the pregnancy? Because if you haven't, I'll back you up and say it's mine."

He said it like he was Mr Darcy, trying to save the day or something. I followed his expression with my eyes, knowing full well it didn't lie.

"I feel exceptionally protective of you," he repeated.

I thought I would melt right there and then on the spot. This guy was just so perfect, and I couldn't believe my luck. I knew I should be saying yes, and falling into his arms, but I was so young and naive … and *almost* innocent. I looked into his pleading, blue eyes, trying to comprehend what kind of a man he really was.

"I can only guess that maybe your mind doesn't work the same way as the rest of the boys in this town, because *no one* would stick by me and support me like you are," I lectured.

"All I want to know is what you are thinking, even if it sounds insane." Ashley played with my hair, maybe hoping it would relax me and I would give him the answer he craved.

"Well, I haven't been able to sleep much. I feel better today though, because there is no longer a baby. No pregnancy, nothing."

He caught it this time. "You miscarried?"

"Yeah, yesterday."

He looked alarmed. "I'm so sorry I've stayed away. Are you … is everything all right now?"

"I went to see the doctor this morning," I confessed, being completely honest.

"I'm so sorry I've neglected you. Some superhero I am, huh?"

"I was distracted all weekend, worrying about you," I added, trying to console him.

"Worrying about me, when you had all this going on? You amaze me!"

"Aren't I allowed to worry about you, then?" I enquired.

"Don't you see, Anna? It's one thing for me to make myself miserable, but another thing entirely for you to be so worried about me, when you should have been thinking about yourself!"

"Just allow me to worry about you if I want to, and I'll worry about worrying about myself later – I promise!"

"You take everything so coolly. It's unnatural…makes me wonder what you're really thinking."

"Don't worry, it's a mask. It's my way of blending in!"

"Everyone at school wants to know if we are secretly dating. Being home today you wouldn't know about all the comments I've been getting. So, shall we make things more official? Anna, *please* answer my original question?"

❧ Fifteen ❦

"So you want to know how I feel about you. Hadn't you noticed?" I was breaking all the rules now, as our bodies melted together in the tenderest of embraces. His full lips caressed mine, tongues dancing in delight, as we exchanged a mouth-watering kiss.

"Now you should know how I feel about you," I confirmed. "And as for your question…well, it's yes to an engagement, but let's put the marriage thing on hold for a few years?" I blushed again, but ever so slightly this time.

"Well, at least I know what you're thinking now. I just wish there were some things that you weren't thinking," he replied.

"I'm not saying no to marriage, just not right now," I quipped, reassuringly.

"Can you also answer me another question? Do you truly believe that you care more for me than I do for you?"

"What sort of a question is that?"

"Just answer it."

"Definitely," I said, firmly.

"You don't see me very clearly, you know. I'll admit you're dead-on about the bad things, like my so-called friendship with Nathan, but you haven't *seen* me clearly until tonight, I don't think, have you?"

"Trust me just this once. I care for you *more* than you care for me," I assured him.

"Mind you, from now on, as my fiancée, keeping you safe from the likes of Aimee and the others will definitely become a full-time occupation. She will be gunning for you and me, because Nathan will have had to tell her the truth about the last few days," he reasoned.

Confession time. "Don't worry about her, and anyway, she already knows. She found Nathan with me after…after it happened."

"Orianna! Why didn't you tell me all this?"

"I just couldn't. I thought I would lose you for good," I said, not daring to think about the possibilities of losing him.

"Don't be so silly. I've been really worried. I was lucky to have Philippa, who has been most supportive," he said, as he lovingly stroked my arm.

"That's good," I smiled.

"Nathan, Aimee and all the others are the ones who don't understand why I can't leave you alone."

"I'm nothing special – at all," I retorted.

"Now you are the one who doesn't see yourself clearly. You know, you're not like anyone I've ever known. You fascinate me." He paused for a moment, smiling into my eyes. "Most girls are predictable. But you…you never do what I expect. You always take me by surprise."

"My sincere apologies, I'm sure. I didn't realise I did that to you," I teased.

Disregarding my attempt at humour, he said, "Most of all I want you to be happy. I don't want anything bad happening to you."

"You mean it, don't you?" I asked.

"Anna, I couldn't live with myself if I ever hurt you. You don't know how it's tortured me, staying away from you, even for a few hours. The thought of you, all alone, with what you have gone through...it was intolerable. You are the most important person in my life, as I keep saying...the most important thing to me, ever."

And so I guess by this conversation, we really were in love.

"The blush on your cheeks is lovely. Don't move. I want to kiss you again."

With that, we fell into each others' arms once more.

"Yesterday's fight with Nathan was such a relief for me – if you could have felt the complexity...the confusion I felt about you in the beginning because of them, you would understand," he said.

"I'm trying to understand," I replied, a little overwhelmed by our whole conversation. The conversation interrupted his persistent kisses.

"Are you feeling faint? Or was it my kissing expertise?" He giggled at his joke.

"It's you," I whispered.

"You're intoxicated by my very presence."

"Something like that," I murmured, stroking his arm as he held me.

"I never imagined anything like this...you know, being with you, close, like this. I didn't believe I would ever find someone I wanted to be with other than my family. Talking of families, should your mother know I'm here?"

"No, you're not corrupting me...yet!"

"You trust me?" He asked.

"Implicitly." I giggled again.

"What time is it?" he asked.

"Oh, does it matter? You've been here for ages...it's just gone eight," I replied, glancing at the clock.

"Where is your mum?"

"She takes my sister to ballet and tap classes, straight from school, then they go and have dinner or see a film. It's their quality time together. They'll be back soon."

I switched on the fairy lights above my bed and then snuggled back into Ashley, feeling the warmth of his body against me as I did so. Taking my left hand, he drew it towards him and I was aware of the enormity of his proposal as he gently slid the huge, heart-shaped, solitaire diamond onto my wedding ring finger. I stared at it in the fading light; it looked rather odd as it sat there, winking at me. I raised my hand closer to the lights to examine it in more detail. It must have cost him a fortune. How could I accept this?

"How does it fit?" He asked.

"Ashley, it's beautiful, but how can I accept this?"

"You're worth it," he whispered. "It's a pink diamond, you know, to match the car." I could feel his warm breath as he giggled in my ear.

"Only celebs have pink diamonds," I stated.

"No, they don't, because you have one now. I'd rather marry you than a celebrity."

"Pff! Well, I'm never going to look like one of them – not the way I walk."

"I've told you, that doesn't matter to me. You have a beautiful face, great personality and men who are so shallow as to worry about a disability aren't worth a light."

"Yeah, I know that. I just feel as if my bubble is going to burst or something. Things like this don't happen to disabled girls," I argued.

"They do now! Just shut up and kiss me!" he demanded, pulling me towards him.

When I opened my eyes, it felt like a normal school day, until I looked down at my left hand. The diamond winked at me again, the same as it did the night before…kind of conspiratorially, I thought.

Frantically, I thrust my hand back under the duvet, as Mum entered the room.

"How are you feeling this morning, darling? I looked in on you last night but it was late and you were sleeping. Did you get on okay at the doctor's?"

"Yes, thanks, Mum, fine. A course of antibiotics." I wasn't lying.

"Izzey and I got back late. We went to see a chick flick, and then popped in to see Aunty Jo. I hope you weren't too lonely without us."

"No, I was okay. I had company."

"I'm glad Amelia stayed. See you downstairs for breakfast."

The door slammed shut as she headed off to make toast. I wasn't going to disabuse her – if she thought it was Amelia, then it bought me some time. I wasn't in the mood for her emotional hysteria; I had everyone at school to contend with yet.

I did my normal human stuff – showered, dressed and put a little make-up on. I wanted to leap down the stairs with joy as I thought of seeing Ashley again. Leaping was an impossibility for me, but I still had those feelings of elation and an overwhelming desire to declare my love for him from the rooftops.

Entering the kitchen, I swivelled the ring around on my finger and hid the stone behind my flesh so no one would notice.

"Here's your tea, love," Mum said, passing me my cuppa.

"How was your dancing lesson last night, Izzey?" I asked, sliding into my seat at the table.

Izzey rattled the box of Rice Krispies, as she emptied most of the contents into her breakfast bowl.

"Fab. Mum and I had a really great time."

I was sometimes jealous of my sister's relationship with Mum. They always seemed closer. But I was growing up, becoming an adult, so I guessed that was how it worked.

"What's that on your finger? A new ring?" Izzey was staring intently at my left hand.

"Sssh, it's nothing! Don't say a word. You'll know more later. You'd better not say a word! It was a present, that's all." I hissed, forcing a smile of warning.

"I won't. I won't, I promise!" Izzey whispered. I could see her looking at me curiously, but I decided to ignore her.

I gulped down the dregs of my tea and swallowed the remnants of marmite on toast before grabbing my school bags and heading out of the door.

"Bye, guys! See you tonight." The door slammed shut behind me.

Sitting in the privacy of my plush little car, I eyed the huge pink stone as it glistened in the morning sun. It was stunning; too ostentatious for me, if I was honest, but it was what Ashley had chosen, so, of course, I loved it.

The engine purred as I drove up the hill towards school; the diamond twinkling with every movement of the steering wheel. Pulling up in the car park, my heart almost skipped a beat as I saw my fiancé standing in front of his black Audi waiting for me. Fiancé and Ashley were two words I had not expected to use in the same sentence, but it was happening and I'd better get used to it.

Ashley was waiting to accompany me into school. My concerns about any confrontations were ill-founded when he was with me. His gorgeous eyes were untroubled and he took everything in his stride. Walking at his side, I felt an enormous sense of relief that he was there.

"Hi," I breathed, smiling manically.

"Hello, you." His answering smile was brilliant. "Did you get a good night's sleep, or did the brilliance from that ring keep you awake?"

"Stop teasing." I frowned. "Everyone's going to notice this today!"

"You aren't ashamed of it?" he asked, looking rather disturbed.

"No!"

"Good. Are you still angry?" he asked, manoeuvring me through the crowds, with his arm round my shoulders.

"Definitely," I grinned.

He sighed, joking now. "Will you forgive me, then, if I apologise?"

"Erm, maybe, if you mean it. And if you promise not to do it again," I insisted.

"How about if I mean it *and* agree to fend off the jealous girls who try to nab that ring off your finger?" His eyes were suddenly shrewd.

I considered, and decided it would be the best offer I was going to get. "Deal," I agreed.

"Then, I'm very sorry if I upset you." His eyes shone with sincerity for a split second, which played havoc with the regularity of my heartbeats, and then as usual he turned playful.

"Right. So are you ready for the onslaught of questions?"

I was already well aware of the hordes of students staring. Some were gawping at Ashley's arm around me; some stared at the ring which stood out like a beacon on a hillside, and others were surprised because I was with him. I really didn't care, as we glided gracefully down the corridor. I could hear murmurings, whispers behind school books and laughing. To hell with them all! All I knew was that I felt absolutely amazing and it was all because of him. We exchanged glances as we walked together down the corridor.

Arriving at my class door, he pulled me quickly to him in a full embrace, in front of everyone, including Amelia and Jack, who stared open-mouthed. Ashley's lips met mine, and we kissed passionately for all to see.

"Mr Mason! Put her down! You are not behind the bike sheds now!" a teacher yelled as he walked past.

As we released each other, Amelia spotted the ring, as my arm rested over Ashley's shoulder.

"Omigod, omigod, omigod! Oh, my GOD!" She dashed up, almost knocking us flying in the process. Ashley released me from his embrace. Grabbing my hand, she clenched my ring finger tightly, staring at the ring.

"Is this what I think it is?"

"Ask Ashley," I told her, with a grin.

Ashley nodded at her. "She said yes." His smile would have illuminated the Eiffel Tower. "We're engaged, but there'll be no wedding bells for a while."

"When did this happen?" she asked, still staring at the ring, though, thankfully, she had let go of my hand.

"Last night. Ashley came over, and he asked me—"

Suddenly, the bell rang.

"Right, girls, see you later. If you need me, Anna, just text."

"Okay, I'll see you at break…I love you," I whispered.

"Come on, Orianna!" I was yanked into the room, bags and all, by a very enthusiastic Amelia.

Jack just sat in his seat, indignantly staring at me. Everyone was talking about my ring and the engagement. I could hear some girls in the corner discussing it, even though they tried to whisper.

"What's he doing, wanting to go out with her, let alone getting engaged and marrying her?"

"Yeah, and cripples can't have kids. You'd have thought he'd be embarrassed walking down the street with her."

"Spastics just end up alone as sad old spinsters and batchelors, don't they?"

That did it. I couldn't bear to hear anymore. Tears began to stream down my face. Their comments were humiliating and I needed to get away from them all. Walking as fast as I possibly could, I escaped to the ladies' toilets near my tutor room.

Shortly afterwards, Amelia followed me in. I could see her shoes below the cubicle door as I sat on the loo lid, my face drenched in tears, mascara smeared and lipstick smudged from wiping my eyes. She tried to reason with me through the door.

"They are just jealous, trust me," she pleaded. "Everyone wants Ashley, you know that. Ignore them, they really aren't worth it!"

As I opened the cubicle door, the main door flew open and Aimee stood there, preening herself in the mirror. She clocked my reflection and flew around in a rage to face me, pushing me against the grey walls, pinning me there, so that I couldn't escape.

"You bitch!" she spat. "How dare you tell Ashley that Nathan raped you? You swore to Nathan and me you would say nothing!" She glared into my eyes, her nostrils flaring with fury.

"I swear I didn't say anything," I yelled back.

"How did Ashley know, then?" She was so close to my face it was uncomfortable.

"I was pregnant…"

She cut me short. "What?" "WHAT?" Her face was crimson with rage. "Are you keeping it? Are you after Nathan for cash?"

"No need to worry your pretty little head over it. I had a miscarriage."

"Oh… You are probably lying about it anyway. That's okay, then." She released her hold on me. "Let's face it," she said nastily, "we wouldn't want another one like you, would we? Breeding like rabbits…you disabled people get it all, benefits, new cars, sympathy, you make me sick." Her snarling came from her torment of not having Nathan exactly where she wanted him.

"Yeah, and, of course, you wouldn't mind being like her – NOT! You'd never walk in heels, always be in pain, never be seen as normal. D'you know what, Aimee, you're the freak, not her!" Amelia yelled.

With that, Aimee turned on her Manolo Blahniks and walked out.

"Well done, Amelia. I never knew you had it in you!"

"Neither did I! Are you okay?"

I went to the mirror to apply fresh make-up.

"Sure. She's no big deal. I expected some reaction like that from her. At least she never saw the ring."

"This whole situation was a nightmare, now it's turning into an amazing dream!" Amelia quipped.

"You're not kidding!"

"I never knew Ashley had it in him – proposing like that, I mean," she grinned. "A real knight in shining armour!"

"No, a superhero!" I giggled.

"Do you know who the real superhero is?"

"No?"

"It's God. Well, who would have expected things to turn out like they have?"

"You really think it's all happened because of our prayer requests?" I tried not to push it, otherwise she'd probably start Bible quoting me again. I stared at my reflection in the mirror, checking my make-up and straightening my dishevelled clothes.

"Don't you?" Amelia asked.

"Well, I guess—" The bell sounded for our first lesson.

Amelia walked with me on her way to class. "Did Ashley know about the pregnancy?"

"He overheard Stephen discussing it with Gary Carlisle, the doctor, on the phone, when we were back at Ashley's. Do you remember? Before we came down to the kitchen."

"He's all right about it?" Amelia looked surprised.

"He is, and would have been, whatever I'd decided. It's just a bonus for us both that I miscarried. I think he would have stuck by me no matter what, though." I sounded like the cat who'd got the cream.

"I really believe what Philippa said now, about Ashley, when she described how much he loved you. He must really love you a lot," Amelia chimed.

"I know." My heart fluttered as I said it, gazing down at my pink diamond, just to confirm that I definitely wasn't in a daydream. It sparkled under the bright fluorescent lights. Each time I looked at it, it winked back at me.

Art, with my fiancé! That word would always sound strange. I was only 17 and engaged. I was also elated, as if I'd been walking on air since last night.

I almost danced along the corridor to art – well, sort of. I stared at the portrait on my easel, wondering whether I would look much different when my surname was Mason.

Suddenly everything went dark, as a pair of warm hands covered my eyes.

"Hi, future wifey!" I melted at the sound of his velvet voice.

"Stop it, you! You'll get us into trouble." I didn't want to be off with him, but out of the corner of my eye, I could see Jack glaring at us. He really was not liking this new me – this world Ashley and I were creating. I still wanted his friendship, but how could that be possible, when he despised Ashley so much? Jack didn't even know him, so why was he judging him? Men! I'd never understand them.

I looked at Ashley's amazing representation of himself. "You better get on with your portrait, baby, otherwise it will never be finished."

"I know, but you see, you are very distracting!" he laughed at me.

I was trying to hold it together myself. His very proximity gave me goosebumps. I was going to have to get used to that. To lighten the mood, I flicked some acrylic paint onto his nose, trying to avoid his smart clothes.

"Right, that's it!" he exclaimed. With that, he dipped his brush into his pallet and then brushed some paint on my cheek.

"You two! Stop messing about and get on with your work – don't let your hormones get the better of you!" Mr Ridgeway snapped.

"Sorry, sir," we both chorused and sheepishly, turned back to our work, trying to focus on our creativity. For the whole hour I had to concentrate on my painting, and not him!

"Hey, you! You and your mum are invited to mine tomorrow night for a family meal – I haven't forgotten it's your birthday tomorrow," Ashley shouted back at me, as I hurried down the corridor to my next lesson.

"Listen, I don't want anything fancy. I've got to talk to Mum later. She knows nothing about us, or the engagement. It will all be a bit of a shock, but I'm sure it will work out. I can wrap her round my little finger."

"I'd love to see that!" he quipped.

Jack dashed past us without a glance.

I got on with the rest of the day, most of it textiles, which I loved. All I could think about was how to break it all to Mum. She was going to freak out. Perhaps I wouldn't tell her tonight.

⇜ Sixteen ⇝

I played with the food on my plate, wondering how to open the conversation. Suddenly, Izzey's voice broke into my thoughts.

"Ooh, what's with the ring?" I knew she would land me in it, eventually.

All eyes were fixed on me and my pink sparkler. It was no longer hidden in my palm, but had somehow worked itself the right way up without my noticing.

"Isn't it on the wrong hand?"

"Um, no," I mumbled, still chasing the food around my plate.

"But if it's on that hand, Orianna, it would be an engagement ring," Mum pointed out.

"It is," I said, simply.

"What? You're much too young. I didn't even think you were serious with anyone?"

"You had an idea I was seeing Ashley," I reminded her.

"But … marriage?" Mum coughed.

"No. An engagement." I wriggled in my seat. "I'm not going to jump into marriage, not for years yet."

"That's a sensible idea. We haven't even met him yet," Mum scoffed.

I sensed that she didn't approve. I was very young, after all. But once she met Ashley, I knew she would change her mind.

"What about your birthday?"

"Ashley's sorting all that out," I told her with a grin.

"What do you mean?" Izzey asked.

"We are all invited to his family home for dinner tomorrow night," I enthused.

"But it's your birthday! That's our family time." Mum exclaimed in horror.

"All the more reason to go out and have some fun, then!"

"You have kept this all so quiet, it isn't like you." Mum's voice was choked up and croaky.

"I really haven't tried to deceive or hurt you," I tried to explain. "I never expected anyone to fall in love with me. I never expected to fall in love back." It had never been my intention to hurt Mum in any way, and I told her so.

"Please give Ashley a chance, Mum. I'm sure you'll love him when you meet him," I said, trying to convince her that everything would be okay.

"I hope so! Especially if one day he's going to be my son-in-law." She half-smiled as the accusing look faded away.

"I can't believe you are getting married!" Izzey exclaimed.

"I'm not, well, not for ages yet and before you ask, yes – you can be my bridesmaid."

"Thanks, sis." She grinned at me. I knew that was what she wanted me to say.

My arm was nearly yanked out of its socket as Mum pulled my hand towards her to take a closer look at my ring.

"Wow! That's some rock. I guess the Masons are rich?" She was on about money again.

"I don't know, Mum. It's not my business." I knew a discussion was about to commence.

"It's not the be-all and end-all of a marriage, but doesn't it help?"

I didn't need this. "I'm not with Ashley for his money, Mum. He really does love me."

"I've noticed your change in mood over the last few months, you know. I had hoped you would have told me voluntarily how you felt about him and what was happening."

"I wanted to, but I knew if it went wrong, you'd be upset for me, so I wanted to see if things would turn out right first. I wasn't being underhanded or anything."

Mum sighed, looking at me in despair.

"I love you, Mum, but I can't do that 'you're my best friend rather than my mum' thing. I have more respect for you than that."

That comment lightened her mood and a brief smile danced across her face and was gone.

"I wouldn't want things any other way, darling." With that she got up and wrapped her warm arms around me, enveloping me in her love.

"I'm really proud of you." The smile returned and stayed for the rest of the evening.

"Tomorrow, you are only going to school in the morning, and then you and I will go shopping for a dress to wear for tomorrow night. I'll write a note for you for school, we'll just say you had a doctor's appointment."

"As long as you're sure? What about work?"

"It's been years since I took any time off. I'll take a sickie," she grinned. "They'll never know."

"Best I get an early night," I sighed. There was so much to look forward to tomorrow, it was doubtful I'd get much sleep. I kissed Mum's forehead, said goodnight to Izzey and went up to bed.

It hadn't gone too badly, I reflected. At least she hadn't gone ballistic, or made a scene. I hoped everything would go well tomorrow. But one thing I was absolutely positive about – I was in love with my future husband…completely and definitely unconditionally.

"Hi, birthday girl!" Smiling broadly, Ashley held his arms out to embrace me, as I hopped out of my car in the student car park.

"Hiya, sweetie. Happy birthday!" Amelia flashed me a brilliant smile.

"Hey, Orianna, like, we got something for you!" Jess thrust a small pink box into my hands, before I could respond to anything.

"Couldn't you two keep my birthday to yourselves?"

"No one could keep their 18th quiet…not even you!" Ashley teased.

"I hope you haven't planned anything too elaborate?" I replied nervously. I shuddered at the thought of being centre of attention.

"It's not going to be a run of the mill night. At least, not when Philippa has organised it," he replied as we all began to head off to registration.

"I suppose it won't. I just don't want anything fancy. It'll be bad enough with Mum and Izzey making a fuss." I was wishing all the attention was on someone else.

"Definitely," Amelia grinned.

He gave a huge, over-exaggerated sigh. "Pray, forgive me then, if my family goes over the top with the celebrations?"

I sighed back, but huffily. "Oh, I will think about it if it makes them *happy* to make a fuss," I insisted.

"It will be fun, Orianna," Jess giggled, linking her arm with mine.

"A birthday and engagement party rolled into one!" Amelia was smiling, too. "Ashley mum's invited us all. Just go with it."

"Okay, okay! I give in," I giggled. Did I have a choice?

I considered opening the present, as I played with the little satin bow that was tied around it. Then I thought it would be better to open it at the party later.

Looking at my mates, I realised how lucky I was to have them. They were so loyal. Apart from one.

"Where's Jack?" I asked, looking in Amelia's direction.

"He said he'd catch up with you later. He's at college this morning. Don't worry, he's fine. At least, he said he was."

My smile turned to a grimace. I was angry that Jack was behaving so badly. He was being so childish, putting our friendship at risk. And for what? He always knew there was never going to be anything between us. I didn't want Jack to ruin my day today. At least he couldn't crash the party tonight; he'd never go to the Masons. At least I'd be safe from any aggro there.

"Listen, love, I don't want you missing anything tonight, okay? I'm going to call for you, your mum and Izzey at 7.00. No arguments." Ashley pulled me towards him, insistent, yet playful. "If I don't see you later, I will see you tonight, and that's a promise." With that, his warm lips brushed lovingly against my forehead.

The morning raced by. Loads of my classmates wished me happy birthday. Some noticed the ring and looked a little shocked, but didn't say a word … at least, not to me. I nearly went flying when Aimee shoved past me in the corridor, glaring as she went.

"All right, bitch!" she hissed as she passed me.

Back to normal there, then.

"I heard you tricked Ashley. Did you tell him the baby was his?"

Her question didn't even justify an answer. Looking at her indignantly, I rolled my eyes and carried on walking, leaving her standing there like a lemon. I owed her absolutely nothing.

Heading off to the car park just before lunch, Ashley spotted me on his way to the cafeteria. My heart performed its normal double somersault as I registered his god-like face. He was sooooo perfect.

"Hey, honey! Where are you off to?"

"Mum's taking me out this afternoon to buy something special to wear for tonight."

"That's nice! Enjoy yourselves – and don't forget I will be round to pick you up at seven o'clock, right?"

"We are all looking forward to it," I smiled.

As I got into my car, I felt a rush of excitement at the thought of spending the evening with all the people I loved so much. I hoped Mum would not go over the top trying to come across as someone she wasn't, in order to impress. Izzey was easy; she was always her sweet self and had fun no matter whose company she was in. Activating the CD player, I immersed myself in the melodic tones of Blue; I'd loved that particular boy band when I was younger, especially Lee Ryan. It was too cold for the roof to go down, so I rolled down the window to let some fresh air in.

Mum came through the Bluetooth.

"Darling, are you on your way?"

"Yes, and I'm going to drive us, okay? My treat."

"Great. See you in ten minutes, then."

Seconds later, the phone beeped again and Ashley's name appeared. My heart skipped a beat and I tried to keep my attention on the road as his velvet tones played havoc with my senses.

"I forgot to mention something to you earlier…"

"What's that, then?"

"I love you."

I couldn't say a word. It left me speechless and witless when he uttered those words.

"Are you still there?" He sounded concerned.

"Um, yes. You shouldn't do that to me when I'm driving. You take my breath away…"

"Okay, I'll tell you later when you are just inches away from me – how's that?"

"Sounds good to me," I giggled.

"You don't drive as fast as me."

"No way. So?"

"So I can rely on you to be safe at the wheel of a car," he giggled. "It's when you're walking, I worry!"

"Hey, stop that right now, you so and so!" I shouted.

"You know I don't mean it. See you later, babe. Have fun!"

Mum came flying out in her normal, casual garb, with handbag and coat streaming behind in her wake.

"What's the hurry?" I asked.

"Nothing. I don't want to waste any time. I need to find something to wear, too."

"Yeah?"

"Ashley's sister called. She thought you'd have taken all day off, as it's your birthday. Anyway, she's meeting us in town and wants to come shopping with us."

I laughed. "Oh, I get it. You want to impress, right?"

There was a pause.

"There's someone else going to your party…a single guy. I asked Philippa if her dad had any friends going who were single."

"Oh, Mum! You didn't? You are so going to embarrass yourself, I can see it." I was irritated that she was going to use my birthday and engagement party as an opportunity to flirt. I couldn't take her anywhere!

This whole situation of taking Mum to see the Masons made me feel like I was trapped in a nightmare…that one where you can feel yourself falling, but can't do anything to stop it.

We parked the car and found the rendezvous – a posh frock shop in Bournemouth. Philippa was standing outside, looking as if she'd just stepped off a London catwalk.

"I come here a lot," she grinned as she stepped forward to kiss me.

"This is my mum, Rachael." I smiled. "Mum, this is Philippa, Ashley's sister."

Mum eyed Philippa up and down, not quite sure of herself and then kissed her at arm's length so as not to crumple Philippa's expensive raincoat.

As Mum and I entered the boutique, the sales assistant regarded us with obvious disapproval. It was quite amusing to watch her whole demeanour change as she realised we were with Philippa.

But Philippa didn't miss a detail. "It's no good you looking at us like that, you know, otherwise you are going to lose a big sale, lady! And we are spending *filthy* amounts of cash, so a lot of sucking up would be appreciated!"

I nearly applauded her. "Philippa, you sound just like Richard Gere in *Pretty Woman*."

"I don't care. It's not every day your mum dresses her eldest daughter for her 18th birthday and oversees her engagement all at the same time!"

Mum was a little shell-shocked, as Philippa took over the whole proceedings, ordering the sales assistant around, as if she owned the place. In actual fact, she probably did, indirectly. Philippa and Rose evidently shopped there all the time as the sales assistant was very familiar with Philippa and was unfazed by the shop and its contents being taken over by her.

After much deliberation, I chose a black satin number, similar to a 1950's hourglass dress, and I was in heaven. The fabric had a rich softness that cooled and soothed as it washed over my skin.

Mum went for a red dress, which wiggled with her when she walked, looking like she'd been poured into it. The sales assistant rubbed her hands in glee as the total rang in the cash register. Mum parted with her money and, with our purchases lovingly wrapped in fragrant tissue paper and packed in exquisite boxes, we made our exit, feeling very self-satisfied.

Philippa had also booked us into the local beauty salon for a session of personal pampering, manicures, massages and facials. After all that luxury, we were ready to go home. I even polished my ring, so it winked at me even more brilliantly in the evening sun.

It was exactly seven o'clock when I answered the door. Ashley looked gorgeous, dressed in smart casual, his hair arranged to look "unarranged" and his blue eyes shining with the excitement of the occasion.

He handed me a tiny package wrapped in black and tied with a pink bow.

"What's this?"

"Your birthday present, silly."

"Thanks. I'll open it later, okay?"

"Sure. But you ought to know something…"

He looked serious.

"What?"

"It won't bite you," he whispered, making me giggle.

I had told him not to go mad. I didn't care how rich the family was; I didn't need or want money being spent on me all the time. In truth, I wanted to vanish into the background. Being the centre of attention was really not my thing. I'd told Ashley to pass on to his family that I didn't want *anything*, not even too much attention. Obviously he had chosen to disregard my requests completely.

"Are you all ready?"

I nodded and Mum appeared in the doorway behind me. He smiled, waiting to be formally introduced to her before stepping forward to embrace us both. Mum seemed surprised, but pleasantly so, and gave me a quick wink as he turned to open the car doors for us. He had impeccable manners and I could see that he already had her eating out of his hand.

"Where's your little sister?" Ashley enquired, as he helped settle me in the front seat.

I wasn't sure and turned towards the back seat. "Mum, how's Izzey getting to Witchampton?"

"Oh, er, I think she's being given a lift by friends," Mum said vaguely.

Hmm. That sounded suspicious to me, but I let it go.

The only light came from the headlamps as we drove down the quiet, winding lanes. The moon occasionally peeped out through a hole in the blanket of cloud; otherwise, the darkness was total, all around us. The trees whispered quietly, disturbed from their rest as we passed them. A pair of foxes slinked across the road immediately in front of us, causing Ashley to swerve to avoid colliding with them.

He was concerned, yet unflustered. "Is everyone all right?" His driving style had not improved. It was still slightly erratic and much too fast.

"Is it always this creepy out here?" Mum piped up from the back seat.

"It's only because it's the middle of winter. In summer it's perfectly lovely, with the smells of freshly mown hay and wild flowers, and there are birds singing in the hedgerows. It's quite different then," Ashley replied, smiling at Mum in his rear-view mirror.

"I think it's a bit creepy as well," I mused.

"So what made your dad move from London to rural Dorset?" Mum chimed in. It would be hard to stop her now that she'd started talking.

"Work, Mrs Stewart. And the fact that he's always wanted to live in the countryside," he smiled. "We all love it here. It's quieter, quainter and much more relaxing than London."

"I can see that!" she giggled. "We nearly had road-kill back there!"

"You get used to near-misses." he said. "Badgers are the worst for car damage, they can write a car off, you know, if you hit them head on. They're a dead weight." He laughed. "Oh yes, and alive with fleas, usually!"

We drove on, talking and laughing, and hanging on tightly round sharp bends, until we could see the lamps of the village in the near distance. We were nearly there. I took a deep breath and told myself to relax.

❧ Seventeen ❧

As we pulled up on the gravel driveway, now familiar to me, I could see Philippa waiting for us. She looked beautiful as she skipped forward to greet us, her delicate features glowing beneath her raven hair.

"Are you going to open your presents now, or later?" she asked eagerly, as we made our way inside the house. Mum thrust her way forward, impatient to be formally introduced to everyone. Ashley was as polite as ever and did the honours. Mum gushed over everyone and it was quite amusing to watch her clocking the expensive furniture and the extensive book and DVD collection.

Rose Mason was as gracious as ever. "It's wonderful to meet you, finally," she said, embracing Mum. "Would you like a drink?"

Mr Mason, looking as elegant as ever, before Mum could reply he'd handed her a white wine spritzer.

"My husband, Stephen, and our eldest son, Jon," Rose said.

Stephen shook Mum's hand warmly and smiled. "How do you do?"

Jon winked at me across the room. I hoped he wasn't thinking I was like her. Mum had been trying to ask Stephen about cosmetic surgery before she had even been handed a drink.

"Now, Mrs Stewart, this is a social occasion," Stephen reminded her. "Let's not go into patient consultations this evening!" he teased.

Mum smiled back nervously, realising she could have overstepped the mark already with her exuberance.

Joshua rushed up to me and gave me a huge hug. "So you are going to be my new sister, then?" His cheeks turned crimson, as he realised he'd hugged a girl. He stepped back quickly, sensing that was not the done thing for a 12-year-old boy.

Philippa floated gracefully around the room. A social butterfly, making everyone feel at ease, she offered drinks and canapés. Entertaining was obviously her forte.

"I've got a surprise for you," she whispered to me as the doorbell rang. She danced over to the door to answer it, and there stood Amelia with Izzey, Jess and a very bashful-looking Jack. They were followed by Gary Carlisle, who had been invited by the Masons. He was alone, carrying a magnum of champagne. Mum's eyes shone with excitement as he entered the room. Was it too much to hope that she would restrain herself and let him do the chatting up … assuming that was what he wanted?

He smiled as he came forward to Mum and me. Mum glowed as she took his hand, lingering a little too long as she shook it. Her heavily mascara'd lashes fluttered provocatively and … was it the lighting, or did she actually blush?

Graciously I shook his hand, not forgetting how he had helped me, not so long ago. But I knew he was a true professional and would not to mention anything. Mum led him away by the elbow, and they were soon engrossed in conversation.

"I never knew you were coming!" I beamed at Amelia and Jess. Unsure as to how to address Jack, I just gave him a peck on the cheek and he seemed satisfied with that, for now.

"No, we kept it secret. It was Ashley and Philippa's idea," Amelia said, glancing at Jack, who looked uneasy.

"We couldn't miss your birthday!" Jess exclaimed, surveying her surroundings in awe. She immediately honed in on Jon, but to be honest, she was out of her depth intellectually. I couldn't see a possible friendship starting there.

Ashley held out his hand for mine, as the guests began to arrive. I took it eagerly, feeling safe that he was there. He gave my fingers a gentle squeeze just to reassure me that this evening was going to be fun.

He brushed my lips with his fingertips. "So, is it true that you really don't want a fuss?" he asked as the double doors to the entertainment room were swung open.

"Yes. Why?"

"Just checking."

I had just laid eyes on a huge birthday/engagement cake, which sat regally on a sideboard in this massive cinema/games room.

He looked at me quizzically. "Most women enjoy birthday celebrations and engagement parties."

"I do! I am!" I responded, quickly. "I'm just not used to being the centre of attention."

Ashley smiled as he ran his hand through his tousled hairdo. Philippa and Jess giggled together beside me, knowing full well that being out of the limelight was not an option for me tonight.

All day, I had actually been considering ways of getting out of being here tonight. It would have been enough for me to celebrate the occasion with a quiet dinner for the two of us. But they all wanted to do things formally and meet my mum, so I had conceded. For me, attention was never a great thing, especially as I was prone to falling over, losing my balance or tripping up at any given moment. Who wants the spotlight on them when they are likely to fall on their face? I usually moaned about not being able to wear heels but I suppose in a way, it was a blessing.

Mum was pleased she'd come as she and Dr Carlisle were getting on really well. She flitted about, picking up framed photos and examining family portraits, looking at the paintings on the wall and generally admiring Mrs Mason's taste in decorating. She was probably also admiring the fact that the Masons had a lot of money. I didn't even want to think about how much. Money didn't seem to mean much to them; well, I supposed it wouldn't...not when Stephen could earn it as fast as he did. Ashley didn't seem to understand why I objected to him spending so much money on me, but I knew how hard money could be to come by, having watched Mum struggle with her finances at times.

I didn't resent their having money. I just hoped they appreciated it. I just felt I was unable to reciprocate his generous gifts, except with my love, which I felt was worth far more than money. I was giving Ashley something that money could not buy...unconditional love. After all, there was another point to this evening besides my birthday.

Champagne glasses were filled and refilled and canapés vanished from plates. Philippa had prepared the room and it was perfect. Scented candles created an ambience and their fragrances were delightful. Plates of delicious hors d'oeuvres and little bowls of nibbles were laid out on side tables, and on the main table, next to an exquisite arrangement of pale pink roses, was a birthday/engagement cake finished with bright pink icing. Also on the table was a random pile of presents, all gift wrapped in black, and tied with pink bows.

Stephen led Ashley and me to the table, banging on it with a spoon, asking for everyone's attention. I was relieved that Ashley was beside me, holding my hand tightly as his father then went on to wish me a happy 18th birthday, proposed a toast, inviting me to open the presents.

With all eyes on me, I nervously thanked the Mason family for so kindly hosting the party and inviting my friends and family.

"...and a big thank you to Ashley," I concluded, "because if I hadn't met him, none of this would be happening."

"Time to open presents," Philippa shouted above the clapping.

Ashley picked up the small packet he'd given to me earlier and handed it to me. It was so light, it felt empty.

"Thank you, Ashley," I smiled.

Beneath the wrapping was a tiny box. I rolled my eyes at him, wondering how much he'd spent this time. I flipped the lid open to reveal a pair of pink diamond earrings. They winked at me in the candlelight, then sparkled in unison with my engagement ring.

I gasped at their perfection. "They are truly beautiful, Ashley." I glowed with pleasure, temporarily forgetting my self-consciousness.

"They match your ring," he said, beaming back at me.

Right on cue, his dad banged the table again. "On the subject of—quiet for a moment, if you please, everyone!" He waited as a hush fell on the room again, and looked round at everyone, smiling. He came between Ashley and myself, placing a hand on each of our shoulders. "On the subject of rings, I am very proud to announce that...as some of you may already know, the delightful Miss Orianna Stewart has consented to be my daughter-in-law one day. All I want to say is that Rose and I are absolutely delighted and honoured to welcome Orianna into our family." With that, he raised his glass. "To Ashley and Anna!"

"Ashley and Anna!" Everyone raised their glasses and cheered as Rose, Philippa and Mum came forward to kiss and congratulate us.

I had just begun to open the remaining presents when a commotion was heard at the front door.

Bang-bang-bang! "Ashley?" a rasping voice yelled through the letterbox, "You in there?"

Instantly, Stephen, Jon and Ashley ran to the door and we all watched as Nathan stumbled into the hall, clearly in a drunken stupor.

"Have you *driven* here, young man, in this state?" Stephen bellowed down at him.

"Yezz…um, Mizter…er, Shteeephen!" Nathan's head lolled about and his eyes rolled as he tried desperately to focus.

"Get him in the kitchen and do it whatever it takes to sober him up!"

Jon and Ashley obliged their father, grabbing Nathan by the arms and dragging him in the direction of the kitchen.

Nathan glowered at me on his way past the wide open sliding doors of the games room, then suddenly dug his heels in and began to struggle, trying to reach me.

"How…how could you do this…to me, mate, uh? Beam…beat me up an' then get en…gaged to that *whore*, uh?"

Mum had been watching the unscheduled cabaret along with the others, but hearing that comment galvanized her into action.

"What is that drunken lout talking about?" She started to push her way through the onlookers, to investigate further.

"Shut your big mouth!" I heard Jon say.

"She's not a whore! You tried to lower her standards to your level, that's all." Ashley barked back.

"She was willing…she begged me for it!" Nathan insisted, still kicking and struggling.

"Right, that's enough. I don't care if I am a friend of your dad's, Nathan. You can get the hell out of my house now!" Stephen roared.

Jon and Ashley, with Stephen's help, changed course and manhandled him back down the hallway towards the open front door.

"You can't do this to me! I'm a *Cooper*!" Nathan bawled back.

I saw my chance. Stephen and Gary grappled with his legs and Jon and Ashley held him firmly by the arms. What an opportunity! I confidently strode up to Nathan, stared him straight in his glassy eyes, and slapped him square in the face as hard as I could.

The fire raged within me. "That is what I think of you, Nathan Cooper – you are a coward, a liar and a junkie. Now fuck off out of my life!" With that, I turned on my heel and marched back into the room to rejoin my friends.

Ashley stared after me in disbelief, almost letting go of his vile, now squirming, former friend.

Stephen was also enraged. "I don't care what else you are, but first and foremost, you are a rapist and you are damn lucky, you young swine, that Orianna didn't press charges. Now get your filthy self out of my sight!"

With that, Mr Mason aimed a kick at Nathan's backside, as, with his three helpers, they hurled him through the door, slamming it shut behind him and bolting it in the process.

Mum was frantic by now. "Can someone please tell me what is going on?" she demanded.

Rose put a calming arm round her, as we heard showers of gravel being scattered by Nathan's tyres spinning away up the drive at speed.

"Mrs Stewart, come into the kitchen. Let me talk to you."

Mum let herself be guided into the kitchen, where the kettle was put on immediately, for an all-restoring cuppa. Gary and Stephen followed.

I felt that I should be in there with them as well. "Ashley, what shall I do? I've told Mum nothing. Nothing at all."

"Trust me, Mum will handle it. Stay here with me, it'll be fine." He wrapped his arms around my trembling body and held me close. "Steady, my love," he soothed. "It'll be all right, I promise."

I heard Mum's voice above all the others, panic-stricken, flustered and very loud.

"Rape! What did he mean, rape?"

There was a pause, some murmuring and then more outbursts from Mum.

"She never told me a thing! WHAT? She tried to gas herself?" Her voice became croaky and muffled, and I realised she had broken down. I clung to Ashley, filled with dread at the thought of facing her.

Gradually, the voices died down and the atmosphere became calmer.

Ashley went to talk to Jon. Jess was sitting with Izzey in the corner, horrified at what she had just witnessed. She looked at me, not knowing what to say ... for once Jess was speechless.

Philippa and Amelia came to my side, trying to comfort me. They knew how distressing it was going to be for me to face my mother and explain all the sordid details about the rape, my attempt at suicide and the miscarriage ... as well as my reasons for trying to keep it from her.

But face her I must.

❧ Eighteen ❧

Finally, the discussions broke up and they all emerged from the kitchen. Mum's make-up was smudged, but her dignity remained intact. She came over and embraced me tightly, without a word. Releasing me, she took a step back and searched my face, trying to understand.

"I'm sorry, Mum," I whimpered.

"Why didn't you talk to me, young lady? I would have understood," she whispered.

"How could I? You were so wrapped up in your own life," I reminded her, "and anyway, I got things all sorted. Ashley supported me a lot, as did Amelia and Philippa."

"But don't you see, Orianna? How do you think I feel when you can tell the Masons and your friends, but you can't confide in your own mother? Where have I gone wrong?"

I tried to reassure her that she hadn't failed me. "Ashley's family have been amazing, as was Gary."

She threw Gary a puzzled look, so Rose obviously hadn't told Mum about the pregnancy. That was a relief.

"It's okay, Mum, let's just get on with the party. I'm not going to let Nathan ruin my life any more."

Ashley was still in the hallway with Jon, having a conference. They reminded me of a mafia family during a conspiracy and I didn't like it; it made me wary and nervous.

"What are you up to?" I asked Ashley when he returned to my side.

"Jon and I were wondering if Jack was okay. He disappeared during the kerfuffle and we were worried about him."

I knew that wasn't all they had been talking about, but I didn't want to push it so I let his comments go.

"I'm going to phone him," I said.

"Why?"

"Because he's my friend and I'm worried about him. I pulled my phone from my handbag, and speed dialled his number.

"Yeah?"

"What's up?" I asked.

"You, the Masons, Nathan – I've had enough! I just couldn't stay any longer. I'll speak to you soon, but in the meantime, please don't phone me." With that he ended the call.

Ashley raised his eyebrows in an unspoken question.

I sighed. "He'll get over it, I guess." Life could get complicated.

Mum and Gary were nearby. They stood very close together and Gary's arm was around her waist. They were obviously getting along well, even if no one else was! Had my mum found herself a decent boyfriend at long last? At least someone had enjoyed the evening!

Weeks after my birthday, things finally began to settle down. Mum and I talked so much about what had gone on months before, so that nothing was left unsaid. Her mood swings improved, mainly because she now knew what was going on with me and Ashley and had been getting to know his family; she too was feeling very much a part of things.

There was another reason for her being happier, and that was definitely due to the numerous dates that she found herself going on with Gary, the doctor. At least she was off those awful dating sites; things seemed to be going well for her and I was pleased.

Weeks turned into months; nothing eventful happened. Nathan and Amiee avoided Ashley and me, I think because they were puzzled I'd not reported him. In fairness, I think his father and Ashley's dad had had discussions and they had warned Nathan off me. So all was now calm.

Ashley helped me into his car, being very careful not to disarrange the flower corsage he'd just pinned to the bodice of my dress. I snuggled into the heated seat and began to relax.

"Did I mention that you look gorgeous?"

I grinned. "Yes, several times." I'd never seen him in evening dress before, and the contrast of his crisp white shirt with his dark hair and blue eyes was dazzling; that I could not fault or deny. With both of us dressed so smartly, I felt rather unsettled and nervous.

"I'm not going round to Amelia's any more if her mum is going to dress me up like a Barbie. She has gone a bit OTT, being a beautician and everything," I griped. I'd spent the better part of the day in Mrs Webb's bathroom, a helpless victim, as she used all her professional tricks, even though I complained. Whenever I fidgeted, she reminded me not to be ungrateful, and that when she'd finished I would look like a million dollars! Then Philippa had lent me this dress – a ridiculous, navy blue silk corset-style dress, with a luxury swing tag. It would be more at home in Oxford Street than darkest Dorset. I felt sure that nothing good was going to come of me being trussed up like a chicken.

We were just about to drive off when Ashley's phone rang. He checked the caller ID.

"Hi, Jon," he said warily.

"Jon?" I frowned.

Things had been difficult for Ashley since Nathan's memorable appearance at the engagement party. Ashley held his cards close to his chest, but I knew something was going on, that he and his older brother were hatching a plan.

Something Jon was saying made Ashley's eyes widen in disbelief, and then a huge grin spread across his face.

"You're joking!"

"What's going on?" I demanded.

Ashley ignored me.

"Why don't you let me talk to him? He is going to be my brother-in-law some day!"

"Patience, sweetie, you will find out soon enough." The call had ended.

He waited for a few seconds after dialling another number. "Hello, Jack. This is Ashley Mason." His voice was very friendly on the surface, but I knew him well enough now to recognise a tinge of resentment when I heard it.

"I'm so sorry if there has been some kind of misunderstanding, but Orianna will not be around to see you tonight." He listened to Jack's reply. "Right, well I'll be completely straight with you, Jack. Anna will be busy tonight and unavailable every night from now on as far as you, or anyone else, is concerned. No offence, mate, but she's peed off with your mooning over her. She offered to stay friends but that wasn't enough for you, was it? All you need to know is that *everything* is being dealt with. Okay?"

As he drove off, there was a huge grin on his face.

My face flushed with anger and I could feel tears of rage welling up.

Ashley looked at me with surprise. "Did I offend you? I didn't mean to – but somebody has to take control of these morons around you!"

I ignored that.

"If you are taking me to the pre-exams prom, can't you be nice?" I yelled.

Didn't he know me at all? I was the only one who could deal with my moronic friends. He was subjecting me to this evening, when he knew I couldn't and wouldn't dance. He knew I felt embarrassed, yet persisted in humiliating me. He hadn't anticipated the force of my reaction; that much was obvious.

He pressed his lips together and narrowed his eyes.

"Don't make this difficult, Anna. Tonight is meant to be special for us."

I looked through the car window. "Why are you doing this to me?" I wanted to know.

"What? Trying to have a romantic evening, or ridding your life of hangers on?"

I didn't answer.

"Anna, honestly, you knew we were going to this prom. I don't care if you can't dance, or won't dance. You're mine – we are together. Let's show everyone that, once and for all, and if they don't like it... well, tough. We don't want Jack hanging around us, pining after you. It's our time now. He had his chance with you and blew it! I'm not being nasty, just honest."

I felt mortified now. Firstly, because I'd missed the obvious, and secondly because the expectations of the day had been forming in my mind and I didn't want to be disappointed. Amelia's mum had attempted to transform me into a catwalk model. And my fearful ideas of how the evening would go seemed silly now.

I tried desperately to hold back the tears. I mustn't cry; my face was plastered in make-up. Had she used waterproof mascara? I dabbed gently under my eyes; I didn't want to end up looking like a panda.

"Oh, really! This is ridiculous. Why are you crying?" Ashley's frustration was clear.

"Because I'm angry!"

"Anna—" He turned the full force of his sapphire gaze on me. "What?"

"Just go along with things? Humour me?"

I felt my anger melting away. I was lost when he looked at me that way.

"Okay," I agreed. Unable to glare as effectively as I would have liked, I pouted instead. "I'll go along with it – if it will make you happy!" I grinned, giving in. "Were Mum and Jon and Philippa in on this?"

"In on what?"

"You taking me to the prom alone?"

"Yes, everyone was, including Amelia and Jack. Jack agreed weeks ago, so long as I sorted Nathan out."

"And have you?"

"What?"

"Sorted him out?"

"Nathan? Oh, don't worry, he's going to get what's coming to him!"

"No fights!" I moaned.

"No fights. I promise," Ashley assured me. "I told you not to worry your pretty little head about all this – it's being dealt with." He was confusing me with all his double-talk and I didn't even want to think about what he was going on about.

We parked in the school car park. Nearby were Amelia's VW and Jack's Vespa. Ashley got out and walked around the car to open my door. He held out his hand. I sat awkwardly in my seat, not wanting to move. I was worried about humiliating myself and Ashley when it came to dancing; I knew it was going to be a fiasco. The car park was crowded with girls in gorgeous frocks of chiffon and silk and guys in tuxedos and bow ties; he couldn't exactly force me to get out of the car.

"When you have to deal with morons and rapists, you bravely stand up for yourself. But if I mention dancing… or being on show—" He shook his head.

I gulped. "Trying to dance—"

"Anna, I'm not going to let anyone, and I mean *anyone*, take the mickey out of you – not even yourself. I won't let you out of my sight – not once, d'you hear?"

His comments made me feel better. I thought about being with him tonight, and feeling safe and protected. Maybe it wouldn't be so bad after all.

I smiled up at him. "I hear."

"See? It's going to be great and we shall have a wonderful time," he said softly.

He leaned into the car and wrapped one arm around my waist. I took his other hand and let him help me gracefully from the car. He kept his arm tightly around me, protecting me like a mother hen and lending his support as I limped in my usual fashion, through the entrance doors.

I gazed at the couples parading their prowess in all their glory on the dance floor. I wished it would swallow me up. Some girls looked ravishing in their long, backless dresses, which clung to their enviable curves. Aimee walked in wearing a black satin dress, which showed off the contours of her hourglass figure. Even though she was a *bitch* she looked beautiful beyond belief. Her gown was backless, tight to her calves where it spilled into a fishtail train, and with a neckline that left nothing to the imagination. The huge crucifix hanging round her neck looked incongruous, to say the least. I pitied every girl in the place; the guys would be helpless with her around. I knew my man was safe, though. She didn't interest him at all.

Spotting us, she made her way over. "Hi," she breathed, through scarlet lips.

Ashley chose to ignore her and so did I.

Cringing, I was eventually towed onto the dance floor. I was so nervous that my throat was dry and I could hardly speak.

"I can't dance, Ashley," I whispered.

Panic rose in my chest as I reluctantly followed Ashley.

"Don't worry, I'm going to make you look good." He promised. His expression was one of confidence, but not in an arrogant way.

"Yeah, right. How?"

"Stand on my feet!"

"What? I will hurt you." This was rather puzzling. Now I knew this guy was mad! Almost as crazy as me.

"No, you won't, just do it … I'll hold you." Ashley put his arms firmly around my waist as my feet slid onto his.

"I'm going to hurt you," I repeated.

"No, you won't. Come on, we can at least try."

Hesitantly I held onto him, as he began whirling around the room, slowly at first.

"I feel like a child!" I began to laugh as the whirling got faster. It was effortless for him, but then everything was, apparently.

"You don't look like a child," he murmured, eyeing my cleavage above the cinched waist.

I realised I was actually enjoying myself.

"Okay, you have won me over. I *can* dance, if we do this all night." I giggled. "Don't your toes hurt?"

"No, not when you're happy," he replied.

At that moment, I really didn't care what anyone else thought of me. For once, it really didn't matter. I felt as if I was on cloud nine. I was certain now that this bubble couldn't possibly burst.

Ashley was staring over my shoulder, towards the entrance. His smile had rapidly changed to a look of anger; his face was as hard as stone.

"Now what's the matter?" I wondered, aloud.

I followed the direction of his gaze and made out the silhouette of Nathan in the haze of the coloured lights. He was crossing the floor towards us.

"I'm so sorry, Orianna … for what I did." His mouth moved stiffly, as if he was being forced to apologise.

I couldn't believe what I was hearing, especially from Nathan. He looked very awkward and uncomfortable. He stood impatiently, waiting for a response, his eyes flickering to my face, and then back to Ashley's.

"You are not welcome here, Nathan. Go back to your bimbo." Ashley jerked his thumb in Aimee's direction. I hadn't seen Ashley look so grimly determined as he put Nathan in his place.

"I am sorry," he repeated as he took Ashley's advice and headed back towards Aimee.

But it was too late for apologies. Ashley took out his phone and made a call. He kept his face turned away from me, but I could just about catch what he was saying.

"Yes, he's here right now," Ashley said and then began giving a detailed description of Nathan. "I know he has some on him now; he has been in the toilets, bragging. His girlfriend uses, too." Ashley then began describing Aimee. "...and she has a vial containing the coke in a massive crucifix round her neck. You can't mistake the jewellery, it's unique. If you come up to the school now, you can nab them both." There was a pause and then he went on to give details of the school.

"It's not my business," Ashley muttered. "I'm just informing you there are drugs on the premises. I'm pretty sure, though, officer, that they are the only users here tonight."

"What are you doing?" I grabbed his arm.

"Nathan and Aimee have their comeuppance. I told you I would deal with it."

We carried on dancing, although we were both on tenterhooks until the police arrived and began asking about Nathan and Aimee.

A commotion soon began to kick off, and Nathan was cuffed, along with Aimee. Ashley and I were out of earshot, so we couldn't hear what was said. Nathan glowered at both of us, realising Ashley or I had probably dobbed him in, but, of course, he couldn't prove it. People started gathering in groups near the doorway. Heads bobbed as, staring, whispering and genuinely shocked, everyone tried to get a better view of the 'golden couple' being arrested and taken away at speed in separate police cars.

I looked at Ashley, knowing full well what he had done; there was no getting away from it. Did I care? I didn't give a damn! Nathan had finally got what he deserved, and his bimbo. All was resolved. Now perhaps Ashley and I could get on with our lives.

With the excitement over, the dancing resumed and Ashley led me back to the dance floor. I felt a tap on my shoulder and turned round to see Jack following us.

"Hey, Ashley... Orianna! I was hoping you would be here." He looked both embarrassed and apologetic.

"Hi, Jack." I smiled affectionately at him. "What's wrong?"

He stood in front of us, swaying uneasily from one foot to another. At a guess, he really wanted to avoid this conversation.

He aimed his reply at Ashley. "I concede defeat. You really stitched those guys up!"

"I did?" Ashley retorted. "How was it that I had anything to do with it?" He glanced at me and then fixed his gaze on Jack.

"You must have done! No one else would have stood up to them, apart from you."

"Maybe. Maybe not." Ashley's tone was very matter of fact.

Jack didn't really have a reply to that. He glanced at me, wondering whether I could shed any light on the situation, and then we both looked away, embarrassed.

"You look really pretty, by the way," he added, shyly.

"Thank you."

I could see Ashley's expression harden as he watched the two of us, floundering. Then he withdrew, walking over to the wall, where he leaned, one hand resting in his trouser pocket, still looking at us. I couldn't fathom his thoughts; his face was expressionless. I judged he was being mature by giving Jack and me some space. Nearby, a year-11 girl was eyeing Ashley up speculatively, but Ashley neither noticed nor cared.

Jack looked away again, shame-faced. "Don't be mad with me, okay?"

I assured him I wasn't.

"I assumed, wrongly, that it was Ashley who got you pregnant first of all. Then when he practically abandoned you, I was mad. It wasn't until a few days ago, when I spotted your ring, that I realised he's not the bad guy, is he?"

"No, Jack. Ashley really did stand by me and he saved my life in more ways than one."

He looked directly at me now, responding to the sincerity in my voice.

"If it weren't for Ashley and his family, I'd probably be dead now," I told him.

"Right." His eyes quickly appraised my appearance. "Um, do you want to dance?"

"The lady said no!" Ashley butted in as he stood beside me once more. "I will take things from here, thanks."

Jack drew back, knowing he'd overstepped the mark. "I guess I'll see you around, Orianna."

"Come and dance, Jack?" At that moment, Amelia, possibly sensing an argument, came alongside and escorted him away.

Ashley wound his strong, safe arms around me and we returned to the dance floor. I rested my head against his chest as he masterfully led me around the floor.

"Feeling better?" he teased.

I smooched a little closer in to him. "Yes, now I know what you have been up to."

"Are you still mad with Jack?" he asked, holding me even tighter.

"Not now he's realised what a superhero you are!"

"I'm mad at him, though."

"Why?" I asked, frowning up at him.

Ashley frowned back at me. "He called you pretty. But he got it wrong... you are *beautiful*."

"I think, somehow, Ashley Mason, you may be just a little biased," I chirped.

"I definitely don't think so, Orianna Stewart!"

Then Ashley altered our mood completely as he whirled me expertly through the dancing couples. We passed Jack and Amelia who were still dancing, and watching us curiously. Jess waved briefly as she accosted some unsuspecting sixth former, who could not resist her charms.

Then we were outside, in the car park, all alone. Ashley swept me up into his arms, carrying me across the grass until we reached a bench beside the tennis courts. We sat down and he drew me in to his chest. This moment could not have been more perfect or more right. There was no doubting it. His arms wrapped around me, holding me tight against him... I had the sensation that every nerve ending in my body was a firework ready to explode. The stars were visible on this crisp night and the moon looked down on us from the heavens.

"Today's over," he said, with conviction.

"Not everything has to end, though," I whispered.

"Will you tell me the truth if I ask you something?" His voice was almost inaudible, as he whispered back.

"Don't I always?"

"Just promise you will tell me," he insisted, "if you ever get bored with me and don't want me any more." His glance was kind of sheepish. Surely he should know me by now?

"As if I would ever get bored with you!" I hissed. "You know I'd never leave you, and anyway, why are we whispering?" I couldn't imagine being without him now; it was unthinkable. "I'll be with you for always," I breathed, looking up at him through Amelia's mum's thick, black mascara.

"We are whispering," he replied, "because I don't want to spoil the moment."

I agreed. "It's perfect. We are here for each other for ever."

If Ashley thought I was bluffing, he was very much mistaken. I had already made the decision that I would be with him for always.

"Yes, for ever," he echoed, looking back at me with those bewitching cobalt blue eyes.

Love is…

A beauty of the highest kind
found in every curve and corner of your features,
face and body,
at the centre of your being,
the meaning of my existence.
You are the beginning, the middle and the end.
You are here for me, always.
My best friend.
I belong to you with every part of my being,
you are all I want and all I will ever need.
Nothing less, nothing more.
You complete me.

Phillipa Vincent-Connolly graduated from The Open University with a BA in Humanities with History, and is now training as a textiles/history teacher. She lives with her two young sons in Dorset.